WELCOME TO
HOMETOWN REUNION

Twelve unique stories set in Tyler.

*Where you can find romance and adventure,
bachelors and babies, feuding families, a case
of mistaken identity, and a mum on the run!*

*Join us in America's favourite town and
experience the love and the laughter, the trials
and the triumphs of those who call it home.*

DID YOU PURCHASE THIS BOOK WITHOUT A COVER?
If you did, you should be aware it is **stolen property** as it was
reported *unsold and destroyed* by a retailer. Neither the author nor
the publisher has received any payment for this book.

*All the characters in this book have no existence outside the imagination of
the author, and have no relation whatsoever to anyone bearing the same
name or names. They are not even distantly inspired by any individual
known or unknown to the author, and all the incidents are pure invention.*

*All Rights Reserved including the right of reproduction in whole or in part
in any form. This edition is published by arrangement with Harlequin
Enterprises II B.V. The text of this publication or any part thereof may not
be reproduced or transmitted in any form or by any means, electronic or
mechanical, including photocopying, recording, storage in an
information retrieval system, or otherwise, without the written
permission of the publisher.*

*This book is sold subject to the condition that it shall not, by way of trade
or otherwise, be lent, resold, hired out or otherwise circulated without the
prior consent of the publisher in any form of binding or cover other than
that in which it is published and without a similar condition including this
condition being imposed on the subsequent purchaser.*

Harlequin is a registered trademark of the publisher.

*First published in Great Britain 2000
by Harlequin Mills & Boon Limited,
Eton House, 18-24 Paradise Road,
Richmond, Surrey TW9 1SR*

DADDY NEXT DOOR © Harlequin Books S.A. 1996

Ginger Chambers is acknowledged as the author of this work.

ISBN 0 373 82554 4

110-0800

*Printed and bound in Spain
by Litografia Rosés S.A., Barcelona*

GINGER CHAMBERS

Daddy Next Door

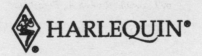

HARLEQUIN®

TORONTO • NEW YORK • LONDON
AMSTERDAM • PARIS • SYDNEY • HAMBURG
STOCKHOLM • ATHENS • TOKYO • MILAN • MADRID
PRAGUE • WARSAW • BUDAPEST • AUCKLAND

WELCOME TO A
HOMETOWN REUNION

Twelve books set in Tyler.
Twelve unique stories.

Romance novels were **Ginger Chambers**'s favourite escape when her children were small, and when she decided to try her hand at writing a book, it was a romance. That was some twenty years and many, many books ago. She's a long-time resident of San Francisco who says visiting Tyler for a Hometown Reunion was like coming home again—revisiting friends and neighbours, catching up on all the latest goings-on. 'It reminds me,' she says, 'of my large family, all the cousins and aunts and uncles getting together after time apart. What fun!'

CHAPTER ONE

WELCOME TO TYLER.

The spring storm was so intense that even with the windshield wipers switched to their highest speed Raine could barely read the sign that marked the town's boundary. Possibly she should have pulled over, waited out the worst of the storm, but she had come so far....

Tyler. The town she had known all her life. The town she once had not been able to leave fast enough. It was ironic that she now was willing to risk life and limb to hasten her return.

She might have been returning to the womb!

A short, sharp laugh burst from her lips.

The womb...

Raine's hands tightened on the steering wheel. She couldn't let herself think about that right now. She had to concentrate on her driving. But how could she not think about it when the fact that she was pregnant controlled her life, dominating every thought, every act, every breath?

It was because she was pregnant that she was racing home. Compelled, in a near panic, to see her mother. To be held in her mother's arms, an inhabitant once again of that magical childhood world where wounds could be fixed with a healing kiss.

A strong gust of wind pounded the car, trying to

ram it sideways. Few people were out on such a horrible night. Since leaving Belton, she'd seen only five
or six other cars and no pedestrians.

She turned off the highway at Main Street, and
shortly, saw the dim outline of the high school where
she'd spent so many long hours dreaming of escape.
Then came some of the shops and offices that clustered around the town square—the town hall, the post
office, the bank. Tyler never seemed to change. Once
she had held that sameness in contempt. It was so
boring here! There was no *life!* She had to break free!
Try her wings! Have room to grow! Now, seen
through anguished eyes, that very sameness offered
relief.

She swung the car onto Morgan Avenue and her
heart beat faster. What was she going to say? How
could she explain? Ever since she'd stubbornly gone
through with her plans to leave Tyler for New York
City immediately after graduating from high school,
a slight strain had existed between her mother and
herself. Her mom hadn't wanted her to go. From the
Midwest perspective New York was a dangerous
place where anything could happen, from physical
injury to tainted ideals. Each time Raine came home
for a short visit, she could feel her mother examining
her, appraising her for change. Raine, of course, dismissed the misgivings. She was fine! She would continue to be fine! And any change in her would be for
the good!

She drew a shaky breath. *Hi, Mom! Guess what?
I'm home, I'm pregnant…and I'm so afraid! Because
as it stands now I'm in this all on my own. When I
told the baby's father, he…* Was that what she was
going to blurt out? Her mother knew nothing of Joel

Hastings, or of the six months they had shared in his apartment overlooking Central Park. It was a secret Raine had kept, not because she was ashamed of Joel or of what she was doing, but because she was unsure how her mother would receive the news. Now the news was even worse.

The final turn was coming up…into the narrow driveway of the small wood frame dwelling on the corner of Morgan Avenue and Second Street, a house Raine had known all her life.

As the car rolled to a stop the wind gave it another hard shake. Overhead, tree limbs jerked and swayed, showering the yard with tender branches and leaves.

No lights were on in the house, but Raine hadn't expected any. Her mother had never been one to stay up late, and Raine doubted that four years of marriage to George Phelps had changed that. All the years of having to be up early to open the diner had formed a habit that would be nearly impossible to break, even when the bulk of that responsibility had been passed on to someone else.

Lightning flashed and thunder cracked as Raine struggled up the sidewalk to the house, growing wetter with each step. Her dress became plastered to her body, her hair soaked, water dribbled down her legs into her shoes. The short porch roof offered some protection and she sheltered beneath it gratefully.

A moment later, after collecting herself as best she could, she rang the bell. No one answered, so she rang it again. Still there was no answer.

Raine swallowed, her emotions slipping ever closer to the precipice. The only thing that kept her from going over was her knowledge that on occasion the bell failed to work. She reverted to a more direct approach.

"Mom!" she called, thumping her hand against the thick wooden door. "Mom, it's me...Raine!"

Nothing. No sound of bare feet padding down the hall, no lamp being switched on to chase away the bleakness of night.

"Mom?" Raine tried again, this time lifting her voice and thumping harder. "Mom...*please!*"

Tears started to mingle with the moisture already on her face. She'd come all this way—left rehearsals without telling anyone, gone back to the apartment when Joel wasn't there in order to pack some of her things, rushed to the airport, waited standby until there was room for her on a flight to Chicago, rented a car, then driven for miles and miles through this terrible storm. Her mother had to be here. She *had* to!

Raine pounded on the door with both her fists, the heavy wood shaking beneath the force of her assault. Then, moving on automatic pilot, she darted back out into the storm to go to the rear of the house.

"Mom! Mom! It's me. Please, Mom! *Please!*" she cried as she beat frantically on the back door.

Still there was no response.

Raindrops peppered her head and shoulders, and sobs racked her body as she sank slowly to the patio's concrete slab. Her once sleekly styled copper-colored hair hung in short wet clumps around her fingers as she buried her face in her hands. She didn't know what she was going to do! She couldn't get in—she didn't have a key anymore. Not since her mother and George had remodeled. And even if she'd been sent a key, she wouldn't have thought to bring it. Not in the emotional state she'd been in when she was packing.

"Raine?"

Someone—a man—said her name in shocked surprise. Raine looked up…into the blinding beam of a flashlight. When, instinctively, she shielded her eyes, the light was withdrawn.

"Raine?" he repeated. "Is that you? What are…" He flashed the light onto his own face. "It's me, Raine…Gabe. You don't have to be afraid."

Gabriel Atwood stood just inside the gap in the trimmed hedge that separated the neighboring yards. Tall and slim, he had the same dark brown hair, cut short, that she'd known from childhood, the same chiseled features.

"Gabe?" she breathed.

She struggled to stand up and he hurried over to help her. Drops of water rolled from his yellow plastic poncho onto her wet dress as he took her arm.

"What are you doing here like this?" he asked, frowning. "Marge wasn't expecting you, was she? She and Doc Phelps aren't here. They're… Hell, this isn't doing you any good, is it? Come on over to our place. We'll talk there, after we get you dried off."

"My suitcase…in the car." Rain motioned to the front of the house.

"I'll get you safe and sound, then take care of that. All right? Are you ready?"

Raine nodded, but when she stepped forward, her foot slipped on a slick portion of concrete, and Gabe ended up swinging her into his arms.

He carried her along the path she'd traveled many times before. Four years of age separated the two of them. Four years that had never seemed to matter.

They'd been great friends all their lives, their relationship shifting and changing many times along the way, but never dissolving. Strong, wonderful, dependable Gabe. Steady as the sun rising each morning.

He didn't put her down until they were inside his house. Raine's sore spirit drank in the familiar sights that greeted her. It was a masculine house, shared by father and son, but it still reflected facets of the woman who'd been Gabe's mother. Raine remembered only small bits about her, mostly that she had passed on her sweet, shy smile to her son, as well as her dark brown hair and clear blue eyes.

"I'm dripping," Raine said apologetically when she saw the water collecting on the rug.

"Just a second," Gabe answered. He pulled his poncho over his head, and after securing it on a hook by the door, disappeared down the hall. He came back unfurling a blanket. "You're freezing," he exclaimed as he wrapped the cover around her.

Raine hadn't been aware that she was shivering. She pushed a thick string of hair out of her face and tried to smile. "It's not so bad," she said.

Gabe looked at her for several long seconds before he drew her to a chair, tucked the blanket cozily around her feet, turned on the television set and went into the kitchen to fill a kettle with water. When he returned he went directly to the front door and shrugged back into his poncho. "I'll need your car keys, won't I?" he said.

Raine dug in her pocket. "The case is on the back seat," she said.

"I won't be a minute."

Raine stared at the television screen once he'd

again braved the storm. A weather advisory was being issued through the Madison station. It warned of continued storm activity on and off throughout the night.

Leave it to her to pick the worst night of the season to decide to come home. And also a night when her mother was away. She should have called ahead, as was her habit...but this time, everything was different. So very different!

The front door opened and Gabe came inside, carrying her rain-splattered suitcase. The smile he flashed her conjured up many warm memories. "Got it," he said. "Now, why don't you change into some dry clothes while I fix the tea? You're soaked to the skin and we need to get you warmed up. Do you think you can make it to a bedroom? If not, I can carry you again."

Raine's smile was more like her old self. "I think I can manage," she said wryly. "I'm not a delicate flower. I slipped earlier. That's why—"

"You look like a delicate flower," he interrupted.

"I'm five foot eight, Gabe. And I weigh...well, never mind what I weigh. It's more than I look."

"Is that the way it is with dancers?"

"That's the way it is with me."

"Let's see you do it, then...walk," he explained when she looked at him blankly.

Raine cast the blanket aside and took several steps forward. "Your room?" she asked. They had spent countless hours in his room as children, playing favorite board games, building plastic models and later listening to records and talking. He'd always had time for her, even when he was busy with sports and numerous other friends his own age.

"Sure," he said. "Or Dad's. He's not here right now, either. I'll tell you about that later, too."

"Are you the only person left in town?"

"I hope not," Gabe said with a laugh. He placed the suitcase on his bed, leaned into the bathroom down the hall and ended by throwing her a couple of large towels. "If you need more, you know where they are." He paused. "Don't dillydally, okay? The tea will be ready in five minutes."

"Since when have you become top sergeant?" she teased.

"Since I found you looking like a drowned rat."

He managed to get the door closed before she could hurl something at him.

Raine's fond smile faded seconds later. With Gabe, it was easy to forget her troubles. He was the closest she would ever get to having a brother. He was always looking out for her. Always taking care.

Tears pooled in her eyes. But not even Gabe could fix the mess she was in right now—pregnant with the child of a man who claimed to love her but didn't want her to keep their baby.

A tap sounded on the door, making her jump.

"I don't hear any movement!" Gabe called from the other side.

"I'm hurrying!" she called back, starting to peel off the layers of wet clothing.

A little less than ten minutes later, after hanging her things in the bathroom, she presented herself in the kitchen. She had changed into warm slacks, a pullover sweater and thick wool socks.

"Have you eaten anything lately?" Gabe asked, his eyes narrowing as he inspected her.

Raine sat at the table where a steeping pot of tea and two mugs waited. "No," she said.

"Do you even remember the last time you ate?"

"They served something on the plane."

"Which you didn't touch."

She looked down. "No."

Gabe settled a skillet on a burner. "Drink some tea and I'll scramble you an egg."

The teapot spout wavered as Raine poured the liquid into a mug. "You want some?" she asked.

"Later," he said.

The hot tea radiated warmth throughout Raine's body. Yet she still continued to tremble lightly—from the chill she'd had, from strained emotion? "I'm not really very hungry," she said.

He delivered the cooked egg. "Eat what you want." He settled into the chair opposite her.

Raine made herself take a bite…then another. She truly couldn't remember the last time she'd eaten. It hadn't been at the dinner she'd attended with Joel the evening before. She'd been too unnerved by the prospect of what she would have to tell him later that night, wondering how he would react to the confirmation of her pregnancy. She hadn't eaten in the hours before that, either, after her visit to the doctor. She'd been too upset.

She winced at the memory and pushed the plate away.

"What's up, Raine?" Gabe asked. His gaze never left her face.

Raine's heart leaped.

Just then a hard gust of wind broke against the house, followed immediately by a loud crash. Gabe jumped up and went to the kitchen window to investigate.

"A big tree limb came down," he said. "It hit the garage."

"This is quite a storm," Raine murmured.

"Worst one we've had this spring." Gabe reclaimed his chair. "Raine..." he said.

He was trying to bring her attention back to his previous question, but Raine wouldn't allow it. Instead, she said brightly, "At least we can be grateful we still have electricity."

"Raine!"

She shook her head, signaling without words that she didn't want to talk about it. "Mom... Mom and George—"

"—Are away for two weeks. They left Friday morning to visit one of Doc's friends in Florida. She didn't tell you?"

There was a long pause. "She—she might have left a message with my service. I...didn't check." Raine's eyes were wide, dazed. "For two weeks?" she repeated. For the second time in thirty-six hours her world received a severe blow.

Gabe nodded.

Raine squeezed her eyes shut. "What am I going to do?" she moaned, not realizing that she'd said it out loud.

Gabe had no idea that she was referring to anything other than her sudden homelessness. "Well, if things had worked out the way your mom planned, I could be letting you into her place right now," he answered. "But they haven't. Your mom was going to leave me one of the new keys so I could water her houseplants, only she must have forgotten, because it's not where it's supposed to be. I moved every pot in the shed and no key. So—'' he smiled slightly ''—your only choice is to stay here tonight. Then tomorrow we'll break a window, if we have to, to get inside. This is more than just an overnight visit, isn't it?''

Raine nodded. It was all she could do not to use Gabe as a substitute for her mother. To fall into his arms and tell him all her troubles. It would be so easy, so natural. But the problem wasn't his. It was hers, and she would have to deal with it.

''You can have Dad's room,'' he said. ''He won't mind.''

Raine frowned. ''You said something earlier…''

''Dad's off on that trip he's been threatening to take for years. He turned sixty-two last February and went out and bought himself a motor home. He's got a new partner at the office, and after the tax rush, he took off for parts unknown. Here…'' Gabe searched among some clutter on the counter and handed her a picture postcard. ''He was in North Dakota last week and plans to keep heading west. He swears he's going to be on the road two, maybe three months.''

''Your father?'' Raine was shocked. ''I never remember him taking more than two days off from work in my life. A week would make banner headlines in the *Citizen!*''

''He was determined this time.''

Just as her mother had been determined to marry Dr. George Phelps. Ignoring convention, they'd eloped shortly after his divorce became final four years before. Her mother had never been one to let gossip sway her. To let other people's ideas about right and wrong affect her judgment. That was what gave Raine hope that she would understand about the baby. Or would she ever *have* to be told? Raine's thoughts raced on, considering the circumstances. If her mother was going to be away for two weeks, the baby could be gone in that short amount of time as well. Erased before anyone noticed.

That was what Joel wanted her to do. Then she could resume her career with little interruption. And who knew? Maybe this time the small part she'd managed to win for herself in the new musical would propel her to the stardom she'd long been searching for. It would be easy to explain away the day or two of rehearsal she would miss.

An abortion would be a quick, quiet, relatively easy way out. Only…was that what *she* wanted to do? At the moment all she wanted was to crawl into a dark hole and pray that she would awaken from this terrible dream.

Gabe gently flicked the end of her nose with a fingertip. "What are you thinking, Red?" he murmured, using the nickname he had long ago given her. "Is it really that bad?"

Raine started. She hadn't realized how long the silence between them had stretched. "It's nothing," she denied. "Nothing at all."

His reply was skeptical. " 'Nothing' doesn't bring you all the way from New York. 'Nothing' doesn't make you look like you've lost your last friend." He paused. "Well, you haven't. I'm here for you, Red. Whatever the problem."

Raine did her best to swallow another onslaught of tears as she gathered his capable hand into her own. "Thanks, Gabe," she said with difficulty.

His clear blue eyes remained steadily on hers, and the warmth of his loyal friendship acted as a balm to her tattered spirit.

CHAPTER TWO

THE STORM HAD TAILED OFF by morning and all that remained as witness to its passage was the debris. Gabe, like many of his neighbors, was outside early to start the cleanup. He began with the largest fallen limbs and worked his way to raking up leaves in both yards—his and Marge's.

He found the top of a child's sandbox as well as someone's lawn chair, all displaced by the wind. A short trip up the street yielded both owners. While he was at it, he checked on old Mrs. Johnson to see how she had fared and if she needed any help. Her granddaughter had already arrived, though, and after a friendly word, Gabe went back to his house.

There was still a nip in the air and everything was very wet. As he sat at the kitchen table, his hands curled around a mug of hot, strong coffee, he felt some of the chill dissipate.

He should probably call the fire station to see if they were being swamped with calls for assistance, but since Raine's unexpected arrival late last night, he was working along the principle of no news is good news. He wasn't going to volunteer. Not today...not when he knew with certainty that something had gone terribly wrong in Raine's life.

A movement caught his eye. She stood in the doorway from the hall, swaying slightly, still groggy, and looking far younger than her twenty-five years. She wore a white terry robe over a pair of pale pink pajamas, her bright hair, cut short and curling under at her jawline, mussed from sleep. All she needed was a teddy bear. And he knew where that was—in her mother's house, on a shelf in the spare room that had once been Raine's room.

"Good morning," he called heartily, trying to cover the concern he'd wrestled with all last night.

"'Morning," she replied. She came to sit across from him, folded her arms on the table and let her head flop on top of them.

"There's no reason you have to be up," he said. "Stay in bed longer if you want. Get some rest. You look like you need it."

"What time is it?" she asked, her voice muffled.

"A little after eight."

"Egad!"

Gabe laughed. "I've already been out and cleaned up both yards."

She lifted her head and leveled her beautiful green eyes on him. "I've always known the people of Tyler exist in a time warp."

"It's called the real world."

"Where I come from some people would say it's the middle of the night!"

"I thought you came from Tyler, like me."

"Well, I do…but not now. I meant… Never mind what I meant. I'm here now."

Gabe waggled his mug. "Want some coffee?"

She shook her head.

Gabe took another sip. He didn't like the way she held herself so tightly, or the look of worried distraction that often pinched her features.

"Are you planning to stick around until your mom comes home?"

"What?"

"Your mom," he repeated patiently. "Are you going to leave before she gets back?"

Her hand fluttered to her throat. "I don't know."

"She'll be upset if she misses you. Are you in between shows?"

"No, I—I have a part, actually. We're just starting early rehearsals."

"Don't you need to be there?"

"Not for a few days... Gabe, do you think we could just drop the questions? I'm not... It's so early..."

He stood up. "Sure. I have a few more things to do outside, then we'll see about getting you into your mom's house. Make yourself at home here in the meantime, though. Everything's still in the same place—cereal in the cabinet, milk in the fridge."

As he started to walk past her she grasped his hand, pressing it to her cheek. "I didn't mean to snap, Gabe. I'm sorry. It's just...right now, everything is so... I don't know what I'd have done last night if you hadn't found me."

"You'd have figured something out. Probably come knocking on my door."

"Still—"

"Don't apologize. We're friends, remember? And friends don't stand on formalities."

"You're the best friend I've ever had, Gabe."

She looked up at him so earnestly that it was all Gabe could do not to fold her into his arms, to use as an excuse his desire to protect her from whatever it was that posed a threat, when in reality, all he wanted to do was hold her. But he'd gotten good over the years at playing his part.

"Sir Gabriel," he said mockingly.

She released his hand, and he had no reason not to continue on his way.

Gabe busied himself in the detached garage, straightening the tools his father had riffled through as he chose the emergency gear he was going to take with him on the trip. Then Gabe checked out the lawn mower, as good a time as any to get it ready for summer. Anything to help take his mind off Raine. Still the troubling questions persisted. What possible reason could have brought her back to Tyler in such a panic? In the midst of rehearsals? And without calling home first? When Raine left town immediately after high school, she'd sworn that one day she was going to be somebody. Someone the town would be proud to call its own. *Lorraine Peterson, Broadway star.* She'd been so determined to succeed, so full of hope and fire. It hadn't happened yet, though. Not in the way she wanted.

He knew the instant she came into the garage. He didn't need the short, subtle clearing of her throat as an announcement. He looked up from what he was doing and set the now-empty can of motor oil on the workbench.

"I haven't seen one of those in so long," she murmured, motioning to the power mower.

"A lawn mower?"

She nodded.

He laughed. "Some around here might envy you."

"You?" she asked.

"I've never minded mowing a lawn."

She had changed from her pajamas into a pair of

jeans and a dark sweater, yet even in the garage's relative dimness, she stood out. She'd always been what Gabe termed one of the earth's "bright" people. Her hair color, her skin tone, her eyes…she didn't need a spotlight to be noticed. She moved with a dancer's grace and power, and he knew from prior experience that it was as easy for her to stand there and gracefully stretch a leg up over her head as it was for him to scratch his nose. Hours and hours of dance class when she was young, combined with as many hours of practice, were responsible—ballet, tap, even some gymnastics. She could sing and act, too. He hadn't been the least bit surprised when a few years earlier she'd finally won a part in a big-time musical production slated for a run in a revered Broadway theater. The part had been small and the musical had closed after only one week, but she'd been wonderful in it. He'd told her so himself after the opening-night performance, on a trip he'd made especially to see her.

"Do you really think we'll have to break in?" she asked, glancing toward her mother's house.

"We could call a locksmith."

Raine had started to shake her head before he completed the last word. "No, I'd rather not. I don't know how long I'm going to stay and if word got out… Is that why you moved the rental car over here last night? So people wouldn't notice it and wonder—"

Gabe moved past her. "Let's see what we can do," he said.

"I'll wait here." She hung back, watching from just inside the garage as he started to circle the house.

People were careful in Tyler, but the occasional

unlatched window wasn't uncommon. The third one he tried opened easily, and he crawled inside.

"Coast is clear," he called from the back door, deliberately muting his voice so it wouldn't carry far.

Raine hurried across the yard.

"I'm not sure if Mrs. Johnson saw me or not," Gabe said, backing out of the way to let her inside. "That bush by her living-room window needs to be trimmed, but I think I saw a curtain twitch." Mrs. Johnson was Marge's closest neighbor on Morgan Avenue, just as he and his father were Marge's nearest neighbors on Second Street. The elderly woman had moved to Tyler shortly after Raine had left for New York.

"She won't tell anyone even if she did," Raine said. "Mom says she worships the ground you walk on. She'll think you had a good reason for breaking in."

"Like checking on a possible fire?"

"Maybe."

The house had a closed feel. Not stale, but lonely; as if it missed its human inhabitants. Gabe watched as Raine moved from room to room, noting the recent additions and changes.

"I like it," she said at last. "It still has the same feel—all warm and cozy like home, yet better. It's just the way Mom always wanted it, only she never seemed able to pull together enough time or the money to do it. Whenever she planned to buy a new stove or refrigerator, or shop for a new living-room set, something always broke down at the diner or she'd lose a waitress and would have to work extra shifts in her place. The diner's needs had to come first." Raine ran her hand along the wood paneling of the recently added study. "Marrying George has been good for her, hasn't it? She's truly happy."

"She seems to be. So does he. The town was a bit surprised when he put his big house up for sale and moved in with Marge here. But after everything that happened—Doc's divorce, his and Marge's elopement—nothing he did was a complete shock. He told Dad shortly after he moved in here that the house on Elm was like a sterile shell, and that living with Marge was like being reborn."

"The people of Tyler do love to gossip."

"Did you think that would change?"

"That's one of the things I like about living in a city. You can do anything you want and no one notices."

"Or cares," Gabe added, and to him that didn't seem an asset.

She shrugged and brushed past him.

As she started back outside, Gabe cautioned, "Let's check a few things." He opened the refrigerator. "Just as I thought. No milk, no margarine." He lifted the lid on the breadbox. "No bread, either. You'll need to get resupplied."

"Like I said, I'm not sure how long I'm going to stay." A defensive edge had crept back into her voice.

"Even if it's only for a couple of days you'll have to eat. Unless you want to share your meals with me…which you're welcome to do. I'd enjoy the company."

"Don't you have to be at the fire station?"

"I'm on my regular four days off. My next shift doesn't start until Wednesday."

"Were you on duty the night of the F and M fire?

Mom told me it was awful, and that it put so many people out of work. I can't believe it was purposely set.'' She shook her head as he joined her to walk across the yard. "Who would do such a thing? It *has* to have been an accident, doesn't it?''

"We're all still waiting to hear what the insurance company rules.''

"What do *you* think?''

"I'm still waiting, too.'' He smiled down at her. "I put out fires, I don't investigate them.''

He opened the back door of his house for her and followed her inside. One quick look showed him that she had used no dishes while she'd been alone earlier. His mug still sat on the table, and the countertop and sink were clear.

"How about I fix us an early lunch,'' he offered, "then we'll make a list and I'll head out to the store. I've learned to make a mean chili. It'll singe your mustache, if you have one.''

"Maybe...another time,'' Raine said, edging toward the hall.

"Why aren't you eating anything, Raine?'' he demanded.

"I...my stomach's been a little funny recently.''

"Are you ill?''

"No.''

"Then at least have some toast.''

She flashed him a resentful look. "Why are you so determined that I eat? You're acting like an overprotective hen, Gabe! Maybe I want to lose a few pounds. Did you ever think of that?''

"Last time I looked hens were female. I'm not female.''

"Stop bullying me!''

"I'm not—"

When she tried to slip through the door he blocked her way. "Stop trying to pretend that nothing's wrong, Raine," he said. "I *know* something is. For the past seven years every visit you've made home has been planned well in advance, and arranged so you wouldn't have to stay longer than a few days. And suddenly you're here—on the spur of the moment, for you don't know how long—and you haven't even told your mother!"

Raine wouldn't look at him. Her gaze slid first to the floor, then down the hall.

"Tell me, Raine," he urged her. "I can help."

She shook her head, denying him closeness. Tears had started to gather on her lashes, and the sight of them made Gabe's stomach twist with fear.

"Has someone hurt you?" he demanded. "You haven't been…" He couldn't say the word. It was something he'd been terrified could happen to her ever since she'd left the comparative safety of Tyler for the mean streets of New York. The late hours she kept, the location of some of the theaters—it all put her at risk.

"No," she whispered tightly, instinctively understanding. "I haven't been raped."

Relief surged through him, but something was still terribly wrong. "Are you in some kind of financial trouble? I've got some money saved…whatever you need, it's yours."

"It's not that," she said.

"A man. A boyfriend." The words hurt him, but he had compromised with reality a long time ago.

She laughed, the sound hollow, empty. "In a way," she admitted. When she turned her lovely green eyes on him Gabe could see the strain and worry churning in their depths.

"You can't do anything about it, Gabe," she said miserably. "No one can, not even my mother. I was just coming to her because—because…" She strove unsuccessfully to keep her voice under control. "Because I couldn't think of anywhere else to go!"

She swayed toward him, and he reached out to gather her into his arms. How many times had he done this in his dreams? Felt her sweet femininity pressed urgently against him? But fact was far different from fiction. In his dreams she wasn't crying with heartbreaking intensity and he hadn't needed to lend comfort.

Tears shook her body for some time, and Gabe didn't try to stop them. Instead he repeated softly, "I'm here, Red. I won't let anything harm you."

"Oh, Gabe," she breathed into his neck, "I wish everyone in the world was as kind as you."

"Now I'm St. Gabriel," he murmured wryly.

Slowly she collected herself, until only an occasional sniff remained.

He stroked her hair, as content as she was for them to say nothing.

Finally, she pushed away. Even after the maelstrom of tears she managed to look beautiful. There were no splotches on her pale skin or puffiness around her eyes. "It's really not your worry, Gabe," she said.

"Tell me," he pressed.

She looked away. "You'll think I'm a fool."

"I won't."

She gave another tinny laugh, similar to the one

she had used earlier, before turning her gaze back on him. "Why not, when I do?"

He waited.

"I'm pregnant, Gabe. The father of the baby says he loves me, but he doesn't want the child. He wants me to…"

She continued to talk, but Gabe lost track of what she was saying. *Raine…pregnant!* A great wind roared in his head, something similar to the storm they had experienced last night. But instead of breaking tree limbs and tossing around possessions, it threatened to crack Gabe's heart.

"Do you love him?" he heard himself ask. He didn't know if he had interrupted her or not.

"I thought I did. I do! Oh, I don't *know!*" She bit her bottom lip in a vain attempt to keep it from trembling. "Gabe, I don't know what I feel about anything! I couldn't stay in New York. Not when… I came here to think. To decide—"

"Who is he?" Once again he heard himself asking a question he would never have posed in a saner moment.

"Does it matter?" she countered.

Gabe forced himself to think rather than merely feel. "You're right," he said and ran a hand over his clipped hair.

"See? I told you you couldn't help…and that you'd think I—"

"He wants you to have an abortion?" he demanded, his emotions hardening into anger against this unknown man.

"It wasn't his idea that I should get pregnant."

"Was it yours?"

"No. It was…an accident."

"But he still had his fun."

"Gabe, don't…please."

Gabe heard the pain in her plea. He went to stare out the kitchen window. He didn't see a thing. Instead his mind raced from one idea to another, trying not to think about Raine and the baby's father, and what the two of them had done in order to—

She tugged on his sleeve, having moved soundlessly across the room to stand at his side.

Words burst out of him. "What kind of a man doesn't want his own child?"

She recoiled as if he'd hit her, and he instantly reached out, dragging her against him, pressing her head to his chest.

"I didn't mean that," he swore brokenly, filled with remorse. "I didn't mean… You have a big decision to make, Raine. And I can't… I shouldn't—"

Her fingers stole up to seal his lips. "Shh," she whispered, tears once again dampening his shirt.

They clung together for a long time, each trying to draw strength from the other.

She moved finally and he unwillingly released her.

"I—I should get my things," she said.

"What for?" He frowned.

"To take over to Mom's."

His frown deepened. "Are you sure you want to do that now? Should you be alone?"

"As you said, I need to think. And what better way to think than by being alone?"

"But…"

"It's what I want," she said softly.

Gabe had no idea what his face revealed to her. Inside, his impulses had scattered. In the end all he could do was nod.

For long seconds after she had left the room Gabe didn't move. Raine was *pregnant!* He couldn't seem to get past that fact.

All the years, all the time they'd known each other... He couldn't remember the actual day he'd fallen in love with her. She'd always been around, tagging after him as they grew up. At times his friends had teased him. But she hadn't meant to cause trouble. Both of them had had something missing from their lives, something they'd found in each other. He'd lost his mother to a freak boating accident, and Raine's father had walked away from his family when she was barely one. Together, they reconstituted a whole.

But love? Boy for girl, man for woman? Had he gone to sleep one night and awakened feeling differently about her? Or had he seen her and realized that something had changed? There was no way for him to pinpoint the moment. The feeling was just there, like the air he breathed.

His private agony was that to this day Raine had never reciprocated his feelings. She continued to look upon him as good old Gabe, friend for life. Almost closer than a real brother. But still a brother, in name if not legality.

"I think that's everything," she said as she returned to the kitchen, carrying her suitcase.

Gabe hastened to relieve her of the burden. "I still think you should stay here. I can take better care of you than you'll take of yourself."

"I promise I'll eat something," she said, smiling tightly.

"I'll go to the store. Bring some supplies over.

Not a lot," he insisted before she could protest. "Just the essentials."

"I don't know what I'd do without you, Gabe," she said and reached out to touch his cheek.

"I'll send my bill over later," he teased.

"Whatever it is," she replied seriously, "it should be more."

The poignancy of the moment was too much for Gabe. He couldn't drag this out much longer. He shifted the suitcase to his other hand and led them out of the house.

"Call me if you need anything," he directed her.

"I will," she promised.

The distance across the two yards was far too short. He wasn't ready to let her go! Yet just as he had stepped back repeatedly over the past seven years to watch her leave Tyler so she could realize her dream, he saw her to the back door of her mother's house and turned away.

What she had told him made no difference to his love for her. He would love her forever, child or no child.

At his kitchen door he paused to look back. She continued to stand in the doorway of the other house, staring at him but not seeing him, a fact he discovered when he lifted a hand to wave and received no response.

She was thinking of *him*—that man in New York. The father of her baby.

As Gabe's hand fell back to his side, it tightened into a fist.

CHAPTER THREE

RAINE SAT CURLED in an overstuffed chair in one corner of the bedroom that used to be her own. A few of her childhood things remained—a favorite doll, a small crystal horse, her teddy—but the area no longer boasted a bed. It had been fully converted into a hobby room, with a sewing machine, work tables and low metal shelves filled to bursting with numerous storage boxes. Bits and pieces of ribbon and cloth signaled projects underway.

Raine held a sample of her mother's handiwork. It was a wall hanging for a new baby that had the child's name, birth date and weight embroidered inside three colorfully appliqued balloons. *Jonathan Alexander Olsen. Saturday, April 21… Eight pounds, four…*

Without a doubt Jonathan had been longed for, wanted. He'd come into the world greeted by beaming smiles and joyous exclamations. Not for a moment had his mother contemplated ending his life before it even began.

Raine placed a hand over her still relatively flat stomach. A child was growing inside her. It didn't seem real!

What kind of a man doesn't want his own child? Gabe's raw demand continued to reverberate inside her mind, along with the way Joel had looked at her when she'd last seen him—as if *she* had done something really stupid, and he had had no part.

"Raine?" Gabe called to her.

She sat up, setting the wall hanging aside. "In here, Gabe! In my old room."

The back door closed behind him as he came inside. "I knocked, but you must not have heard," he called.

A grocery bag rustled as he placed it on the counter. Then he came to find her. "Quite a change, huh?" he said, smiling.

"She kept my old poster." Raine motioned to the beautifully rendered drawing of a pair of ballet dancers superimposed over the enlarged, ghostly image of a swan.

"That's because the girl looks like you."

"I used to dream it was me."

Gabe stuffed his hands in his pockets. "I brought you a few things."

"Thanks."

Seconds passed. Not exactly uncomfortably, but slightly strained. A new experience in their relationship.

"Don't think badly of me, Gabe," Raine said at last.

His look of surprise was genuine. "I could never do that!"

"But to be so stupid!"

He came over to crouch beside her chair. "Don't do this to yourself, Red. Things happen, both good and bad. I see it every day."

"But to let…" She twisted her hands together.

"I've been thinking," Gabe said. "This man…the baby's—" he paused and took a quick breath

"—the baby's father. You told him straight out about the pregnancy? I mean, you didn't just…talk around it?"

"I told him, Gabe."

"And he still…?"

Raine nodded shortly.

"What about the part you're rehearsing? Can you keep it, if you decide to keep…"

Raine gave a watery laugh. "No. I'm cast as a turn-of-the-century ingenue. The two things wouldn't go together at all. I'd be let go."

"How far along…" He stopped, as if uneasy asking such an intimate question. "No—" he shook his head "—that's not my business."

She touched his cheek. "You could never intrude, Gabe. If anyone's intruding, it's me…on you! It—it helps to talk about it, though. To you."

"Marge would be better."

"Maybe, maybe not. It's her grandchild I have to make the decision about." She paused. "It just doesn't seem possible, Gabe. I took care! I tried to make sure he always took precautions, too! And still it happened."

A tiny muscle twitched in Gabe's cheek. She felt it move beneath her hand.

"I want to give you another option, Raine," he said, his blue eyes holding hers. "For if you want to keep the baby."

She couldn't sit still any longer. She stood up and walked over to a worktable. "I'm not sure I'm ready for that, Gabe. The whole idea… I don't have any money, any insurance. I couldn't stay in New York. I'd have to come back to Tyler…probably work in the diner until… And you know how people are here!'' She shuddered involuntarily at the thought of being the object of all the derisive gossip.

"None of that would happen if you married me."

Raine's restless movements jerked to a halt. "Marry...?" she repeated.

"Just in name. Not in...you know."

She shook her head. "No. I won't do that to you, Gabe. I got myself into this mess, I can get myself out."

He walked over to her. "With an abortion," he said.

"I don't know! I don't want... But—"

"How far along are you?" This time he completed the question. "Nothing shows."

"A little more than ten weeks."

He thought for a moment. "That would work out just right. I went to a training course in mid-February, then I took the next week off for a short vacation. Gossips here could count all they want."

"Gabe—"

"Think about it, Raine. That's all, just think about it. It's another option. I don't want you to feel like you're backed into a corner with no escape."

"But Gabe, it would be so unfair!"

"Aren't I the one who has the most to say about that? And afterward? Well, we can end it whenever we want after the baby's born...when you've had time to get your life back under control and can decide what you want to do with the future."

"But what about you? What about your life?" she countered. "What would it be like for you to continue living in Tyler? It's too much to ask, Gabe. Having to put up with all the speculation, having to put up with me being pregnant. So far I haven't had any trouble, not even bad morning sickness, but that doesn't mean everything will continue smoothly. Then, when it's over—when you've seen me through the worst—all you get is a quick thanks?''

"It wouldn't be the first time." He gave that sweet, special Gabe grin.

Raine stared at him. "You really mean it, don't you?" she murmured huskily.

"I've never meant anything more in my life."

She frowned. "Why?"

"Taking care of you is a habit. It feels kind of funny when you aren't around."

"You find plenty of people to fill in. Mom's told me how much you do for the town."

"Just think about what I said, okay?"

She nodded and he turned away...leaving the room, leaving the house. Leaving her to do as he suggested: think.

RAINE CONSIDERED the situation from every possible angle, until her emotions became hopelessly ensnarled. She wanted the problem to go away! Yet she shied away from the act that would ensure its disappearance. She wanted Joel to have reacted differently, to want both her *and* the baby! But merely wanting it did no good. If she let herself have the baby, everything she had worked so long and hard for would be derailed...for a year? Two? Three? If she didn't, if she aborted, she could resume her work right away. Return to the production company, be ready with the others for tryouts in the regional theaters, and then later on, be there when the play opened on or off Broadway in late fall. *Late fall.* That was the doctor's estimate of the baby's due date.

Raine closed her eyes and groaned. A decision would have to be made, and made soon. Pregnancy was one of those few instances in life when the passage of time only added to the complication.

Instinct pulled her both ways. Her brain voted for the stage; her heart, the child. She speculated about who the baby would look like. Would it have Joel's black hair and dark eyes? Or be filled with color like herself?

And how, currently, did she feel about Joel? She hadn't been able to answer Gabe's earlier question. Nor could she answer her own now. The wound was still too deep and fresh to poke and prod.

Then there was Gabe. Steady, dependable Gabe... with his ready solution to rescue her.

Raine fought with the dilemma all night, trying to find the right answer. The result was that she slept far later into the next day than she'd planned. She awoke, dragged groggily from a frightening dream that didn't want to end, to someone pounding on the back door.

"Just—" She choked on the word and had to start over. "Just a minute!"

She searched for her robe but couldn't find it. Finally, as the pounding continued, she stumbled down the hall wearing only her pale pink pajamas.

Gabe stood on the back step, his expression anxious.

"Is something wrong?" she asked, opening the door.

"Where the heck have you been?" he demanded. "Were you asleep?"

"Yes."

"It's two o'clock in the afternoon! I thought..."

She pushed tousled hair away from her face, waiting for him to continue. When he didn't, she examined him more closely. "You thought what?" she asked. Then realization struck her. "You thought that I... Gabe! I'd never do something like that! I was *asleep!* I didn't... Last night wasn't very easy for me. I stayed up late thinking, like you said."

He looked away from her, to a car passing on the street. To hide the fear that Raine could still easily see in his face?

Her flash of indignation melted. "I didn't mean to worry you," she said quietly. "I had no idea what time it was, or that you'd be concerned."

He shrugged dismissively, but he still didn't look at her.

Raine frowned, then became aware that the top two buttons of her pajama top were undone, and that the resulting gap revealed far more of her right breast than she would ordinarily expose. "Oh!" she murmured and quickly righted the problem.

Gabe stuffed his hands in his pockets and chanced a quick glance her way.

For some reason Raine blushed. Because of the inappropriateness of what he'd seen? Because of embarrassment over what he'd previously thought? Because of both?

"I came to ask if you'd like to have dinner with me tonight," he said, "or, I guess for you, lunch. I promise I won't make chili. It'll be something light and nutritious."

"You sound like a chef," she teased, striving hard to bring them back to their usual footing.

"It goes along with being a fire fighter," he said.

"Is that what you big he-men do all day? Sit around the station and talk about recipes?"

"We're liberated." He grinned.

"I think it's more that you just like to eat. You want to come in? Have some coffee?" She moved back a step so that he could enter.

He shook his head. "I have some things to do. That's what I originally came to tell you. I'm going to be out for a few hours this afternoon. If there's anything you need that I haven't—"

"I'm fine," Raine interrupted. "In every way except one."

"You're remembering what I said?" he asked.

"I'm remembering," she said. He started to turn away, but she stopped him. "Gabe, I truly am sorry I worried you."

Another slow grin spread across his lips. "A few more minutes and I might have called up reinforcements."

"The rescue squad?"

"No, an ax...to break down the door!"

"I can just imagine how much Mom would appreciate *that!*"

"She would if it was necessary."

Raine didn't miss the ring of truth behind his reply. "Yes, well..."

He smiled and gave a little wave before walking away. A minute later she heard a car start up in the garage next door and soon a late-model, dark blue Ford Explorer backed out of the drive onto the street.

Raine spent a moment wondering where he was going. To visit a friend? A girlfriend? Considering the closeness she felt to him, she knew very little about his adult life. Her only information came from the small nuggets gleaned from her mother.

A huge yawn overtook her and she turned back into the house, planning to make herself the cup of coffee that she had offered him.

THAT EVENING Raine gave the dual sets of quick taps on Gabe's door that had long been the private signal between the two households. Even their parents had come to use them, having been taught by their children.

Gabe answered the door and saw her inside. The aromas that greeted her were wonderful.

"Vegetable soup and sourdough bread," Gabe announced when she asked.

"You made bread?"

"No, all I supplied was a pan and the oven. But I made the soup."

"I'm still impressed."

"Wait till you taste it. Are you ready to eat? Or would you like to wait?"

"I wasn't very hungry before, but now…yes, I'm ready to eat."

Gabe seated her at the table, where two places had been set and where a vase with a single sprig of bright yellow forsythia blossoms, cut from the hedge separating their two yards, served as a centerpiece. After ladling soup into two bowls, he settled across from her and motioned for her to begin.

Raine took a small sip. The flavors bloomed in her mouth. She lifted an eyebrow and took another sip. "Mmm. This is very good, Gabe," she exclaimed.

"It's Chief Sorenson's specialty. Mine's the chili I told you about yesterday."

"Chief Sorenson...*Ed* Sorenson? Becky Sorenson's dad?"

Gabe nodded. "He became fire chief about two years ago. He's a good man. Knows what he's doing."

"And Becky?"

"She's doing something with helicopters in the army. I think she's stationed at a base in Texas."

"Becky?"

Gabe grinned. "She's learning to be a pilot."

"Becky?" Raine's repetition was even more incredulous. "But she's afraid of heights. When we were in school together, she got nosebleeds on the second floor!"

"She must have gotten over it."

Raine shook her head, remembering the quiet, frail-looking girl who had had a secret crush on Gabe for years and who had always envied Raine her free and easy relationship with him.

"How long has she...?"

"Two years. She wants to be a career soldier."

"I'm almost afraid to ask about anyone else."

"You remember Mitch Reynolds?" he asked.

She nodded. Mitch had been one of Gabe's best friends.

"He's out in California, doing some pretty amazing things in computer software technology."

"He always was smart."

They both ate more soup and pulled pieces off the sourdough bread.

Raine looked at Gabe curiously. "Do you ever wish you'd left Tyler, Gabe?"

"What for?"

"To see something different. To be with other people. To, I don't know, see something of life!"

"I have everything I want right here. I like the people. I like my job. Tyler's a good place."

"But it's so…" She searched for the properly derogatory word.

"So much the same?" he completed for her. "You always did think sameness was boring. But I kind of like it."

"But you're a fire fighter! Surely every fire's not the same."

He laughed. "No. You have me there. Each fire has its own personality."

"I never knew you wanted to be a fireman, Gabe."

"I never knew it myself."

"Then what made you decide?"

"One day I just walked into the station and asked how to become one. It seemed like a good idea at the time."

Raine stared at him, stunned that someone, especially Gabe, could have fallen into a career choice so haphazardly. To her, that was tantamount to opening the yellow pages, closing your eyes, sticking in a pin…and wherever it landed, that was what you did with your life! She'd dreamed of being on the stage forever. She'd prepared for it, one way or another, almost from the cradle. There was never any question about what she wanted to do. Yet look at her. Here she was, back in Tyler, her prospects for the future bleak.

Her good-natured veneer crumbled. She could continue putting her difficulties to the back of her mind, trying to pretend that everything was normal, but that didn't mean that it was. She had a problem. She had a *big* problem, and hiding from it wouldn't solve anything.

Gabe reached for her hand, which had stopped, frozen, in midair. Gently, he guided the full spoon back to the bowl. Then he curled his fingers around hers and gave them a sympathetic squeeze. He said nothing. What could he say?

"I wish..." she began, but didn't finish.

"What do you wish?" he asked quietly.

She bit her bottom lip and looked down at the table. "That I knew the right thing to do."

"Some people would say you don't have a choice."

"Have the baby, you mean."

He nodded.

"Are you one of those people, Gabe?"

He shook his head. "No."

"Yet you..." She stopped again. This time he didn't press her.

The litany of alternatives tumbled once again through her mind—the numerous difficulties she would face with either choice; all the "what-if's" for years to come. She could see herself at some point in the future, looking back. Would she be happy with the decision she'd made? Or would she long to turn back the clock in order to whisper a better answer into her younger ear?

Raine would be the first to admit that she wasn't particularly religious. She never had been. So religious considerations didn't enter into it. For her, there was only her own sense of fealty, of duty.

She looked at Gabe and saw the man he had become...after being raised by his father, alone. Then she looked deeply within herself. Her mother had raised her alone, too. Neither of their parents had taken the easy way out when tragedy or trouble visited early in their lives. They hadn't run off in pursuit of a dream. They had stayed where they were and worked with what they had, doing their very best for their children.

Raine had long ago acknowledged that she wasn't made of as strong stuff as her mother. She'd been the child who'd been taken care of, who had been abandoned by one parent, but not the other. Her mother had given her twice the love, twice the encouragement. Could Raine do anything less for her child-to-be? Beginning with the most basic decision of all—whether to let it be born?

"Gabe?" His name on her lips broke the long silence.

He looked up from a contemplation of the tabletop.

"Does your offer still stand?" she asked. "Are you still willing to marry me?"

He grew very still, his blue eyes riveted on her face. "Yes," he said simply.

"Then let's do it. I—I want to keep the baby."

A pleased light entered his eyes and his hand on hers tightened.

REVEREND SARAH Fleming Kenton was not the sort of person to ask many questions, which made her the first person Gabe thought of when it came down to choosing who would marry them.

"You'll like her, Raine," Gabe said as he pulled the Explorer into a parking space across from the stark brick building with its high steeple and the sign out front stating Tyler Fellowship Sanctuary. "She came to town about four years ago and has really settled in. She lost her first husband—he was a minister, too—but some months ago she married again. To someone…well, a bit unexpected in the role of a minister's husband, not to mention in some other quarters in town."

Gabe could hear himself droning on, sounding for all the world like a lonely old gossip. He kept thinking that at any moment Raine would pull out, change her mind, come to her senses. The ink on the marriage license was barely dry from their trip to the county courthouse in Sugar Creek, and here they were, already on their way to the ceremony. Sarah had told him she had a half hour of free time available that morning, and Gabe had quickly jumped at it.

He chanced a glance at Raine. She was quiet, very quiet. She hadn't said more than ten words since he'd called for her earlier that morning. He couldn't tell what she was thinking. Her face revealed nothing.

But she was beautiful in a pale yellow dress of some kind of soft material, simple in design, yet a striking contrast to her bright hair and pale skin.

"Turns out he's a Baron," Gabe continued as he collected her from her seat and closed the passenger door. "A son no one knew Ronald Baron had. He showed up around the time of the F and M fire. For a while people thought he had something to do with starting it. But it turned out that he didn't."

Gabe wasn't sure if she was listening to him or not, which might be just as well. He clamped his jaw shut in an attempt to stop himself from talking.

He, too, had taken special care with his clothing,

wearing his best dark suit. It wasn't every day that a guy got married. Even if it was supposed to be pretend. Even if he wasn't supposed to love the bride.

He glanced at Raine again, wondering if he'd spoken out loud. It was that kind of time, that kind of moment where everything seemed to speed by on one level, yet move in slow motion on another. He'd experienced that same phenomenon in the midst of battling a fire, when tongues of flame flicked dangerously close.

When Raine caught his look and smiled, a short, tight, grateful effort, he had a moment's pause to wonder if he was doing the right thing by her. He wanted to help her, not—

Reverend Sarah hurried across from the parsonage to meet them at the side door of the church, her robe billowing out behind her. She was a small, slim woman about the same age as Gabe, with dark red hair, golden-brown eyes and a liberal array of freckles. She shook hands with him and smiled at Raine when he introduced them.

"I've heard so much about you from your mother," the minister said. "I'm glad to finally meet you. Is it just the two of you?" she asked as they entered the church.

"Just us," Gabe replied.

"We'll need a couple of witnesses. Mrs. Williams is here, and I'll see if I can catch Michael before he leaves. Unless…" She stopped to glance at Gabe. "That is…if it's all right with you?"

Gabe's work with Reverend Sarah was carried out mostly over the telephone, when she alerted him to people in special need of assistance. He knew her husband far less, but was aware of the town's lingering distrust. "No, it's fine," he said after what he hoped was only a short pause.

Sarah smiled and hurried away.

Gabe and Raine sat down on a pew. When Gabe took one of her hands, it was like ice. He laughed and rubbed it, but he wasn't sure his were much warmer. "We should have stopped for some flowers," he said.

"Gabe? Who's Michael?" Raine asked, confirming that she hadn't taken notice of what he'd said earlier, or, for that matter, what he'd said just then.

"The reverend's husband."

She nodded.

Suddenly he leaned forward. "Raine, if you want to change your mind—"

The side door swung open and Sarah entered the church, her robe once again caught by the wind. Directly behind her was a nondescript woman in wire-rim glasses and a tall, dark-haired man, who had the Baron good looks, only with a rougher edge. The robe settled as the door shut.

Sarah made the necessary introductions, then had them come to the front of the church, where she positioned them and started the ceremony.

It was over in less than ten minutes...and felt as if it had happened to someone else. Gabe had given his replies, Raine had given hers. But when Sarah told them they could kiss, that they were now man and wife, Gabe was momentarily flummoxed.

His hesitation was embarrassing. He knew he wasn't responding like a normal groom. He wasn't sweeping his bride into his arms and sealing their union with a triumphant kiss. He could sense Sarah's puzzlement, her curious look. So he quickly leaned down and slid his lips across Raine's cheek.

Raine, too, looked slightly dazed, but she accepted his gesture with a tremulous smile.

Then Sarah and Michael and the church secretary were congratulating them, and it seemed natural to grin and wave and hurry out of the church.

Back in the Explorer, Gabe sat very still, as did Raine in the seat next to him. They had done it and he was glad, but it hadn't been as he'd hoped—if he ever allowed himself to hope. The ceremony had been quick and bloodless, and as they now sat side by side, there was no real joy.

How did she feel? What was she thinking? He looked at Raine. Tears were welling in her eyes, ready to spill over onto her cheeks, and Gabe's heart gave a hard twist. The marriage wasn't at all what she had wanted, what she had dreamed…because *he* had never been a part of her dreams.

Without a word he started the engine, and when it caught, he backed the car out of its slot and set off in the direction of their homes.

CHAPTER FOUR

A LITTLE WORD HERE, a little word there...news about the wedding spread quickly through Tyler. Julia Innes had been on her way to drop off her daughter at TylerTots, the day-care center in the basement of Tyler Fellowship Sanctuary, when she'd seen Raine and Gabe come out of the church. She'd recognized Raine instantly even though it had been some time since she'd last seen her. She mentioned her observation to Patricia Sikes, who, dressed for her exercise class, was dropping off her younger son. Patricia mentioned it to her friend Marcia at the exercise class, who later, in a seemingly offhand way, mentioned it to Reverend Sarah during a meeting both attended. Sarah told her about the short ceremony, not suspecting the barrage of telephone calls her news would unleash.

THE SIMPLE GOLD BAND weighed heavily on Raine's finger. It had been Gabe's great-grandmother's ring, his mother's mother's mother. Raine remembered seeing it when she was a child, when Gabe had shown her the special box his father kept in his top bureau drawer. Gabe had gotten into trouble for doing it, but he'd never told that she'd begged to be allowed to see it. Gabe's great-grandfather had bought the ring in France while serving in the mili-

tary during the First World War, and Raine had
burned to touch something from so far away. Now it
was hers, on her finger, and she felt such a fraud.

Immediately after the ceremony she'd known that
she shouldn't have done it, that she shouldn't have
taken advantage of Gabe's good heart. She'd wanted
to rush back inside the church and demand that the
minister take everything back. That she dissolve the
fledgling union, even if it was only in name. Gabe
had looked so dejected when she'd finally let herself
glance at him. Had he just then realized the gravity
of what he'd committed himself to?

Another awkward moment had occurred immediately after Gabe pulled the Explorer into his drive.
He'd invited her to his house, but she'd refused. She
could tell that he didn't really mean it—that he
needed time on his own, just as she did. Later they
could come together and talk, but at that point the
ceremony was still too close, the promises to love,
honor and cherish.

Someone knocked on the back door, drawing
Raine from her reflection. She assumed automatically
that it was Gabe, forgetting to use the private taps.
But it wasn't. When Raine opened the door, it was
Patricia Sikes who stood on the patio.

Raine recovered quickly, even though the visitor's
identity was a jolt. She kept her smile in place. "Patricia!" she exclaimed.

"So you *are* back in town!" Patricia cried, reaching out to give her a quick hug.

"Yes...yes, I am," Raine agreed.

Patricia's eyes were bright with interest. "I heard,
but I just couldn't believe it! You and Gabe! I wanted

to be the first to congratulate you! Am I? Am I the first?''

Raine's heart sank further. Word was out, not only about her return to Tyler, but about the marriage. "Yes," Raine confirmed, "you are."

Patricia tried to peek beyond Raine into the house. "Is Gabe here? I thought you both might be over at his place, but when I didn't get an answer there, I came over here. I wanted to see you quickly so I wouldn't interrupt…well, you know. I didn't, did I?''

Raine had known Patricia Sikes when she was still Patricia Matthews, long before she'd married Richard Sikes, the insurance man's son. Raine and Patricia had never truly liked each other, although both pretended differently on the surface, for the sake of small-town convention.

Raine's fingers tightened on the doorknob. "As a matter of fact…" she began. Let Patricia think what she wanted, then maybe she would leave.

"Well, I won't stay," Patricia said in a rush. "All I wanted was to say hello." She tipped her head. "I suppose this means you're moving back to Tyler? I can't imagine Gabe going to live in New York. Are you, ah, planning to start a family soon? I have two children now, both boys. They're a handful, let me tell you, but I wouldn't trade them for the world. My suggestion is that you should start a family right away. Why wait?" she finished brightly.

Her entire line of questioning had been dripping with distasteful curiosity. It was everything Raine could do not to slam the door in her pert, petty little face. She watched as Patricia hurried away, obviously bursting to pass on the information she'd gleaned.

"Who was that?" Gabe asked. He had crossed the yards without Raine noticing.

"Patricia Matthews, or rather, Sikes. She wanted to know if I'm finally going to admit I have no talent, and to see if I'm already pregnant."

"She asked you that?" Gabe was incredulous.

"In her own way." Raine pulled him inside, just in case Patricia might look back. "Gabe, the whole town's going to know about the wedding by morning."

Gabe smiled slightly. "I expect it will. It's not something we can keep a secret. If it was, there'd have been no need to—"

"But I didn't want it to happen yet! I wanted... We need time to get used to the idea ourselves."

"It's probably best to get it over with. You can't hide in your mother's house forever, Raine."

"But it will look so... And you—"

"You aren't going to give me that bit about my reputation, are you?"

His blue eyes danced and Raine made herself relax. What he said was true. The news had to come out sooner or later.

"Where were you just now?" she asked. "Patricia said she tried your place first. You weren't hiding in your house, too, were you?" she teased.

"Getting you this." He brought out the hand he'd been holding behind his back. "A woman should always have flowers on her wedding day. Even if the wedding..." He stopped. "They're a little late, but..."

"Oh, Gabe, they're beautiful!" Raine exclaimed as she accepted the small bouquet of pale pink roses.

The blooms were buds, barely open, still waiting to fulfill their promise.

He shrugged, but she could tell that he was pleased by her reaction.

She rummaged in a kitchen cabinet for a vase, filled it with water and added the flowers. She touched one of the creamy petals and looked at him, her eyes alive with affection and gratitude. For the flowers, for all that he had done.

"There is one thing," he said a moment later. "If people know we're married...isn't it going to look funny if you stay here?"

"Is it?" she murmured, but she already knew the answer. Marriage to Gabe provided a refuge, but it also brought with it certain expected behaviors.

He nodded. "You can use Dad's room...at least until he comes back. After that, we'll find someplace else to live. The housing market in Tyler is wide open right now, what with the F and M being shut down. Lots of people are putting their houses up for sale."

"I don't want to deprive you of your home, Gabe."

He chuckled. "You won't be depriving me. I'm right at thirty years old. I should have my own place by now. It's unusual that Dad and I get on so well we can stand to live together."

"Still—"

"Stop worrying. We'll face that problem when we come to it."

Raine suddenly frowned. "What am I going to tell my mom, Gabe? I hadn't thought before, but... And what about your dad? Do we tell them the truth or—"

"Let's don't worry about that right now, either."

Raine agreed, but she remained uneasy. Her mother would see through their falsehood in a second. She knew her daughter far too well to be put off by any kind of pretense. Raine might be able to fool other people when she wanted, but she could never fool her mother. There weren't enough acting classes in the world for that.

Raine traveled back across the yards, Gabe following close behind her with her suitcase.

As they passed the rental car parked in his drive he said, "I'll turn it in for you later this afternoon, if you like. I'm going to Sugar Creek anyway, and I'll have a friend bring me home."

"Thanks," Raine murmured. She held on tightly to the small vase with the pink rosebuds. So much had happened so quickly. If she thought about it too long or too deeply at this point, it could easily overwhelm her.

They went into the house and down the hall, to Charles Atwood's bedroom. Here the presence of Gabe's mother, Denise, was more pronounced. The room still retained a definite feminine touch, from the collection of delicate porcelain "Lady" figurines on the mahogany vanity table to the fine Nottingham lace doilies that protected the surface of the matching nightstands and bureau. Denise Atwood had been a discriminating collector. She'd bought only what she loved. And after her untimely death her husband had been unable to part with anything she'd chosen. Raine hadn't fully understood his reasoning when she was younger. Now that she had matured, she sensed that when Charles Atwood entered this room at night, he returned to the loving heart of his wife.

In here, even after twenty-three years, something of her still lived.

"Are you sure your father won't mind?" she asked, turning to Gabe.

"If we had a spare room, we'd set you up there. But since we don't..." He smiled. "Anyone else, Dad might mind. You? He won't mind at all."

Raine examined one of the porcelain figurines. The woman's dress was caught billowing in the breeze, while a tiny dog played at her feet. Her face was pensive, strikingly beautiful. As children, Raine and Gabe had been forbidden to play in Charles Atwood's room, and they'd respected that order, except for the one occurrence.

The wedding band gleamed as Raine put the figurine back in place. "I'll be very careful," she promised.

"We're grown-up now, Raine," he murmured.

"I know, but I still wouldn't want to break anything."

Gabe smiled in understanding, then he turned to survey the room at large. "We'll make space in the closet and empty a couple of bureau drawers. You don't exactly have a lot of clothes, do you?"

She looked down. "I left in a hurry."

"You'll probably want to get some new things."

"I'm going to *have* to get some new things...later on."

"What about a doctor?" Gabe asked, following her line of thought. "An obstetrician."

"Is Hank Merton still at Tyler General?" Her eyes fluttered shut. "This is like some kind of terrible nightmare, Gabe! What am I doing here? How could I possibly have let this happen? How could I...?"

She didn't finish, but she knew Gabe would have no trouble completing the thought. *How could I have married you?* But she didn't mean it in the way it would sound, as if he were somehow lacking.

She glanced at him, and when she saw the telltale tightening of his jaw, she crossed over to him and placed her cheek against his shoulder. "I don't know what I'd do without you, Gabe," she said softly, trying to make amends. "I'm so afraid sometimes. I'm afraid to watch my body balloon, I'm afraid of the actual *birth,* I'm afraid of being a mother...*me?* I'm afraid of being alone...."

Some of the tenseness left his body, and he began to stroke her hair, softly, sweetly, reassuringly.

"You'll never be alone, Raine," he said.

She snuggled closer, grateful for his strength.

THE TELEPHONE RANG several times that afternoon. At each instance Raine braced herself for prying questions, but each call had been for Gabe. Twice he'd left the house and been gone for at least an hour. Both times when he'd come back he'd brought her little presents.

"You need cheering up, Red," he'd explained.

One present was a key chain, on which he'd hung copies of the key to his car as well as a key to his house. A bright green four-leaf clover encased in clear resin also dangled from the chain. "For luck," he said.

The other present was a goldfish, which swam in a small glass bowl.

"I tried to find one that looked like Fred," Gabe said, recalling the fish that Raine had won at a fair as a child and loved for many years. "But this guy…" He shook his head.

"Maybe this one's a girl," Raine suggested, smiling as she peered into the bowl. Gabe was doing everything he could to make the situation easier for her. It was the least she could do to play her part. "Let's call her Frederica," she suggested.

Gabe straightened. "What if it's not a girl?"

"What if Fred wasn't a boy? I never knew, and he never minded."

"Frederica it is, then," Gabe agreed.

The telephone rang again and Gabe groaned. It had been an eventful day. Raine knew he had to be tired. "Do you want me to tell them you're not in?" she volunteered.

He shook his head. "It might be the station."

But it wasn't. She knew that from the funny look that settled on his face seconds before he said bracingly, "Dad!" and turned away from her.

A lively conversation ensued, and not once did Gabe mention her. After hanging up, it took him a moment to turn around.

"How is he?" Raine asked.

"Fine."

"You didn't tell him," she stated quietly.

Gabe rubbed the back of his neck, a gesture he often made when uncertain. "I couldn't. He's still in the Dakotas. If I told him now, he'd come straight home. And that's not what we want—at least, not yet. Not to mention his ruined vacation…"

"I agree."

"But he's not going to like it when he does find out."

"Tell him when he's far enough away—in California or Oregon," she suggested.

"He's still not going to like it."

"Yes, but by then he'll have had most of his vacation."

Gabe relaxed enough to smile. "Since when have you learned to be so devious?"

"From all my years of survival in New York."

Gabe's smile held, but Raine sensed that it was forced. Because New York reminded him of her predicament? Because he didn't think that she had "survived" particularly well? To divert his mind she leaned forward and spoke to the fish. "Where shall we put you, Frederica?" she asked. "How about over there on the table by the window?"

"Do you think she needs a view?" Gabe asked dryly.

"Everything needs a nice view, even a fish." She moved the lamp a little to one side to make room for the bowl.

"You're going to be a good mother, Raine," Gabe said as he watched her work.

"I hope so," she said softly.

"You will," he insisted.

GABE WENT BACK on duty at the fire station the next morning. He'd warned Raine before they separated the night before that his shift was for twenty-four hours—from 7:00 a.m. to 7:00 a.m. He'd gone over his entire work schedule with her, showing her the calendar where he kept track of his days. One on, one off, one on, one off, one on...then four straight days off, after which the cycle started all over again. He'd also made sure she knew where to find the nonemergency telephone number of the fire station, and told her to call anytime she wanted. She'd listened, nodding, but he could tell that she was having a hard time staying awake.

Before leaving that morning he'd left her a note, repeating his schedule and telling her that since it was his usual practice to walk to work, she had free use of the car.

Gabe strode easily down the street, listening to the sounds of Tyler as the town came awake to the new day. The air was cool and fresh, with a light touch of spring. Birds twittered in the trees and a few daffodils were starting to bloom. Here and there he could hear snatches of conversation, as well as the cry of a baby wanting to be picked up.

A baby. Raine's baby. His and Raine's baby? He shook his head in fierce denial. His only role in this arrangement was one of support! He couldn't let himself think beyond the pregnancy to the living child! To his relationship with the child. To his continued relationship with Raine.

He knew he was treading on dangerous ground, that he was opening himself up to tremendous pain— exactly what his father would have told him if he'd known. Which was another reason Gabe hadn't told him about the marriage. His father had long ago guessed Gabe's true feelings for Raine. And he would worry about him…about them.

The usual joggers ran by as he skirted the town square. As was habitual, he exchanged brief greetings with each. Other people he knew waved from cars, off to an early commute to their jobs in Madison or Milwaukee.

At the fire station the previous shift, consisting of

four fire fighters—some paid full-timers, some volunteers—was preparing to leave as the new shift of
four straggled in. Coffee and rolls were available for
all in the dayroom, encouraging them to mingle.

As Gabe entered the big living room/kitchen combination, his co-workers, who had been either seated
at a long dining table or sprawled on couches and
chairs watching the morning news on TV, greeted
his arrival with shouts and whoops of jubilation mingled with moans and groans of frustration.

"Hey! I won!" one cried.

"Me, too! I told you Gabe'd be here!"

"Dang!" someone else grumbled.

"Come on! Pay up! Gimme my five!"

Gabe knew instantly what was happening, but he
pretended ignorance. "What's up?" he asked, strolling over to the counter to help himself to a cup of
coffee.

"Wait a minute...*wait!*" one of the losers cried.
"Maybe it's not true. And if it's not, all bets are off!
Nobody wins, nobody loses."

Gabe took a sip of hot coffee and leaned back
against the counter. "Have you people gone completely nuts?" he asked.

Several of the group approached him. Maureen
Wilson, a solidly built young woman with sharp fea-
tures and short, silvery-blond hair, was first to speak.
"We've heard something," she said.

"Yeah, and I, for one, don't believe it," Bill
Nance exclaimed, butting in. "You, married? To
Raine Peterson? How could you be married to Raine
Peterson when everybody here knows she in New
York?"

"Do you have a question?" Gabe asked.

"Yeah," David McGregor, one of the losers, snapped. "What's the truth?"

Gabe took another sip of his coffee before he said, "It's true."

For a moment all present were stunned. Then shouts broke out and five-dollar bills were snatched from unresisting fingers.

"Then what the hell are you doing here?" David McGregor demanded, his bushy eyebrows forming a straight line as he frowned. "Why didn't you call in sick or something? Isn't this supposed to be your honeymoon?"

"To Raine Peterson?" Maureen Wilson echoed, ignoring David's questions.

"But she's in New York!" Bill Nance tried again to understand.

"She's come back," Gabe answered.

"But—"

Chief Sorenson poked his head out of his office. "What's going on out here?" he asked with deceptive mildness.

"Gabe's got married, Chief!"

Gabe could tell that the information wasn't new to Chief Sorenson. He'd heard the rumors as well. "To Raine Peterson, right?" the chief asked as he strode over to thump Gabe on the back.

"Yes, sir," Gabe confirmed.

"Well…congratulations," he said, then he seemed to run out of words. Finally he asked, "You, ah, want some time off?"

Gabe was prepared. "Not now," he said. "We just want to keep things quiet for a while. Take things easy."

The chief said gruffly, "Well…just let me know if you change your mind."

Gabe's co-workers continued to hover after the chief went back to his office. They were obviously bursting with questions, but reluctant to pose them. Gabe knew he would feel the same way if the situation were reversed.

"She's quite a looker," said David McGregor, a recent addition to Tyler. "From the pictures I've seen hanging in Marge's Diner," he added lamely in explanation.

There were nods all around, then Maureen said, "I didn't move to Tyler until the tenth grade and she was a year ahead of me, but I remember she was nice. We were in a couple of talent shows together."

"Talent!" one of the other fire fighters teased. "What kind of 'talent' did you have, Maureen? Don't tell me that caterwauling you do could be called a 'talent'!"

When Maureen turned to defend her singing voice, Richard Jensen, Gabe's closest friend inside and out of the department, tapped his elbow and motioned for him to follow him downstairs. They went to stand by the huge red fire engine, where Richard used the pretext of showing Gabe a worn spot on a hose. Richard was just coming off duty and would be going home soon.

"This just doesn't seem right, Gabe," Richard said, his dark eyes filled with concern. "You never said a thing, and I saw you yesterday."

Gabe shrugged. He'd wanted to tell Richard when he'd asked him for a ride back to Tyler from Sugar Creek after returning the rental car, but he hadn't been able to find a way.

"I also heard another rumor," Richard continued levelly. "It's pure speculation at this stage, of course, but—"

"I imagine you have."

"Is it true, too?"

Gabe had first met Richard Jensen when they started training together six years earlier. More than once during the intervening years, they'd taken turns saving each other's skin in ticklish situations. Gabe knew he could trust Richard with his life, just as Richard could trust him. But there were some things a man just didn't tell another man.

"Is it yours?" Richard asked, taking Gabe's silence as agreement.

"Who else's?" Gabe quipped.

"I've heard you talk about her," Richard said slowly, "but I never thought..."

"I love her," Gabe said, and his simple statement rang with such sincerity that Richard had to believe him.

Still, Richard seemed to sense that Gabe wasn't telling the entire truth, that some essential element was missing. But he chose not to press him further. Instead he extended his hand, his rugged features rearranged into a half smile. "Then I should be offering my congratulations, too, instead of giving you the third degree. If anyone around here deserves to find a little happiness, Gabe, it's you."

Richard was four years Gabe's senior and lived in Sugar Creek. He had a wife and a son that he never saw because his wife had disappeared with the boy several years before. The half smile was about as much levity as Richard seemed capable of these days. And what he said meant a lot to Gabe.

"Thanks," Gabe said. Then, to lighten the moment, he said, "You'll have to come meet Raine. Have dinner with us."

"In a week or two," Richard murmured.

"Yeah," Gabe agreed, realizing again a little too late that he wasn't acting like a brand-new bridegroom who would rather not have people visit. "In a week or two."

Richard held Gabe's gaze for another second, then he turned to leave the station.

As Gabe started back upstairs to the dayroom, he braced himself for what was to come. People were full of curiosity, and not all of them based their interest on concern, like Richard. In the days ahead Gabe knew he was going to be met with questions from every direction—at the station, whenever he went out on call, as he carried out his regular duties, in his free time.

Under normal circumstances a marriage between himself and Raine would shake up interest. But done like this? They might as well have hit a hornets' nest with a hockey stick!

CHAPTER FIVE

RAINE MOVED restlessly to the couch, where she plopped down to click on the TV with a remote control. A talk show sprang instantly to life, its guests gesturing wildly as they argued. Raine changed channels. Another talk show, another argument. She changed channels again. This time a big purple dinosaur was dancing with a batch of singing children. She switched off the television. She didn't really feel like watching, anyway.

She got up and went to a front window. Outside the sun was shining, a woman was walking her dog, a young child rode by on a bike. Raine sighed. She wanted to be out there with them, *doing* something. Her body was unaccustomed to such a long stretch of inactivity. But she shied away from leaving the house. Word of the marriage had spread like wildfire.

The telephone had rung so many times that morning that Raine finally had been forced to leave it off the hook. Declarations of surprise and offers of congratulation were all too often followed by prying questions and the occasional catty remark. *Did Marge know? What about Charles? He wouldn't have left on vacation if he'd known, would he? Gabe was such a sly one...no one suspected.* Or: *I knew it all the time! I always suspected the two of you would get together!* After two or three calls Raine had wanted to scream!

What they needed was an answering machine in order to screen the serious calls from the merely curious. She couldn't have done without her service in New York, catching word of callbacks, preserving messages about upcoming tryouts, intercepting her mother's calls during the time she lived in Joel's apartment....

Thinking of Joel only increased Raine's restlessness. The way he had looked, the things he had said... He'd hurt her badly. She hadn't meant to complicate his life. She hadn't meant to complicate hers!

Joel was like quicksilver in an already fast-paced world. He was a fascinating man, a charming man, complex, volatile. A wonderful dancer and choreographer. He'd taken her breath away in the first seconds of their initial meeting. Women loved him. He'd had his pick. And he had chosen her.

All along she'd known he had a somewhat undesirable reputation to go along with his many theatrical successes. He used people, friends had told her. Took what he wanted and discarded them when they were of no further use. She'd put their warnings down to jealousy. If he hurt people, he didn't mean to do it. He had to make choices. And sometimes it was those *choices* that hurt people, not him! It distressed him when others accused him of being callous. She'd defended him, supported him. Only, when she'd found herself in need of support, he'd shown a side of himself that she had never seen before.

"Raine? Raine, it's me! Britt," a muffled voice

called through the front door. "I know you're in there! I talked with Gabe."

Raine lifted her head, blinking. "Britt?"

"Come on! I won't bite, I promise."

Raine opened the door and Britt Marshack spilled into the room. She didn't look at all like the mother of five children, the oldest of whom was sixteen and the youngest—a new addition with her new husband—only two. As was her usual habit, Britt had attempted to subdue her mass of strawberry-blond hair into a single braid, but a goodly number of shorter hairs had escaped to curl rebelliously around her smiling, freckled face. It was a face that, at that moment, Raine wholeheartedly welcomed.

"My goodness, are you expecting a siege?" the new arrival teased. "I thought I heard the sound of a bar lifting. Not that I blame you. You certainly are the number-one topic of conversation around Tyler today. I was only in town five minutes before someone rushed up to give me the news. I didn't believe it at first, then someone else told me, and someone else.... So I went searching for Gabe and he confirmed it." She looked at Raine carefully. "Raine...what's going on? I saw your mother Friday morning just before she left for Florida and she never said a word about you coming home, or about you and Gabe, or—"

Raine interrupted their old family friend with a quick hug. "Hello, Britt," she said, smiling. In Raine's opinion Britt was one of the dearer residents of Tyler. She was sweet and kind and always attempted to see the good in people before looking for the bad.

Britt hugged her back, then, chagrined by her own

lack of manners, said, "How terribly rude I've become. My only excuse is that things are just so hectic in the business right now. You know we've opened a Yes! Yogurt shop in Tyler."

"Mom told me."

"Well, it's doing great, but every single day another problem seems to crop up. That's why I came into town today. To deal with one."

"How are Jake and the kids?"

"Fine, just fine. You haven't seen Jacob yet, have you? He's absolutely the most adorable two-year-old on the face of the planet, but I might be a tad prejudiced. He looks just like his dad. Blond hair, brown eyes…"

They settled on the couch.

"You'd just found out that you were pregnant the last time I was home," Raine said.

"I thought it had been that long." Britt frowned. "Raine…"

"Mom doesn't know," Raine said.

Britt's frown deepened. "The marriage wasn't… planned?"

Raine knew that she could tell Britt anything and it would go no further. But she owed it to Gabe to keep up the pretense. "No, Gabe and I didn't want a fuss."

"I didn't know there was a 'Gabe and you' to fuss about. At least, not like that."

"You said you saw him earlier?" Raine asked.

Britt's frown cleared into a smile. "He looked a bit frazzled, but I guess that's understandable, considering how he was on his way back to the station after giving a fire-safety demonstration to a class of preschoolers."

Raine smiled as well. Gabe would be wonderful with children.

Britt echoed the thought. "He'll make a great father...one day."

The slight pause told Raine that Britt had heard the other rumor, as well, but it wasn't something she was going to ask about. Her sentiment concerning Gabe had been natural, not used as a probe.

She stood up. "Well, I can't stay. Jake was expecting me back at the farm an hour ago. Which reminds me, could I use your phone? Just to let him know I've been delayed? Otherwise he'll worry."

"Of course." Raine motioned toward the telephone on the desk.

Britt crossed over to it. "The receiver's off the hook," she said, glancing back curiously.

"Too many good wishes," Raine said dryly.

Britt grimaced. "I can imagine."

The call took only a moment and Raine soon was accompanying Britt to the door. She thought about asking her to stay for dinner, but talk would inevitably return to recent events, and Raine wasn't ready yet to discuss them with anyone, not even an understanding friend.

A SHORT TIME LATER the telephone rang again, startling Raine with its unexpectedness. When Britt had finished her call, she must have forgotten to leave it off the hook, and Raine had failed to check.

She stared at it, of two minds whether to answer. What decided her was Gabe. From what Britt had said, he too must have been getting bombarded with questions and comments, and if it was him trying to reach her...

She lifted the receiver on the fifth ring, but didn't get to say anything because the caller's anxious voice burst into her ear.

"Gabe! Thank goodness! It's me, Marge. Listen, I only have a minute. George's friends are waiting for us. They're taking us out on their sailboat for a few days, and I just realized that I forgot to leave you the key. In fact, I'm looking at it right now. That's how I realized... Gabe?" Her mother's tone underwent a subtle change, as if it had suddenly occurred to her that she might not be speaking to Gabe. "Gabe, is that you?"

Raine's throat was so tight that she could barely answer. "Mom?" she said huskily.

There was silence on the other end, then, "Raine?"

"It's—it's me, Mom," Raine confirmed.

It didn't take a trained ear to detect that something was wrong. Emotion had swept over Raine the instant she heard her mother's voice. Frequently while growing up she had resented her mother's rules, her way of doing things. They'd clashed, they'd butted heads—particularly about her move to New York. Her mother had wanted her to be satisfied with doing theater work within the state. But at this moment, nothing in the world was as sweet or as dear to Raine as her mother's voice.

"Raine?" Marge repeated sharply. "You're at Gabe's? What's happened? What—?"

Raine wiped away the moisture that had spilled over onto her cheeks. She strove to hold herself together. "Nothing's happened, Mom. Everything's fine. I—I just...came back for a visit."

"Then how come you don't sound fine?" Marge demanded, not fooled for a second.

"I just... I—"

"And why are you visiting now? You never come home without letting me know first. New York isn't exactly a hop and a skip away. You can't just drop in for a coffee."

Raine could say nothing more.

Neither, for a moment, could her mother. Then Marge stated firmly, "George and I are coming home. Right now. You can deny all you want that something is wrong, but I know better. We'll catch the first plane that we can."

"But your visit..." Raine whispered.

"To heck with our visit! We're not having that much fun anyway. These people used to know George when he and Mary were married. I don't quite fit the bill for them. They're nice, but I can tell."

"Mom," Raine blurted out, "Gabe and I are married."

There was another long silence. "Tell me the rest when I get home," Marge instructed, just before she hung up.

Raine pressed the disconnect lever with her finger and very carefully laid the handset down on the desk to prevent it from ringing again. All the while a thick haze of tears continued to blur her vision.

She hadn't wanted to do that. Now her mother's flight home would be fraught with worry. But Raine didn't want her to hear the news from someone else, which could easily happen the second she set foot in Tyler.

GABE REQUESTED and received permission for a quick trip home. He knew he would have to suffer knowing looks and ribald comments from his cohorts, but his concern was such that he was willing to endure it. He'd tried numerous times to contact Raine, and at each attempt he'd gotten a busy signal. As the afternoon wore on, he'd started to worry.

Gabe stepped inside the house. "Hey, Raine, it's me!" he called.

The house was quiet. Too quiet. Then he saw her, sitting very still on one corner of the couch, a damp tissue crumpled into a ball in her fist. Relief surged though him, only to be followed by a resumption of his previous concern.

He hunkered down beside her, assigning the couch arm the duty of keeping him from drawing her into his arms. She looked so beautiful sitting there, so sweet and vulnerable. A spark of physical desire shot through him, which he quickly subdued.

"What are you doing here?" she asked softly, reaching out to smooth her fingers through the short hairs above his left ear.

"I came to check on you," he answered honestly. His smile didn't come easily. "All I've been getting were busy signals. Now I scc why." He indicated the disabled phone across the way.

"We've had a lot of calls. Gabe," she said, frowning, "it would help if we could get an answering machine. I have a little money left. I'll be glad to—"

He went to the hall closet and rummaged inside. "I have one," he said. "I set it up for a while, but Dad hated it. He told me to put it away or he was going to pull it out by its roots and throw it out the door." He came back with a telephone/answering machine combination and quickly made the exchange. "He says he hates talking to a machine, so he's not going to make anyone else do it."

Raine smiled tightly. "I would have liked to have that option earlier."

"I'm sure."

"No, I mean I *really* would have liked to have it earlier. Mom called."

Gabe's attention was caught. "What did she say?" he asked.

"She and George are coming home...right now, immediately. I had to tell her that we were married, Gabe. I couldn't let her come back and have someone else—"

"Did you tell her why?" he asked.

"No. We're going to talk more when she gets here." Raine started to twist the already abused tissue.

"They could be home tonight," Gabe murmured.

"Probably. For sure tomorrow morning."

"Would you like me to take the rest of this shift off? The chief offered—"

Raine shook her head. "No. It's better if I talk to her alone." She looked at him. "I'll have to tell her the whole truth, Gabe. I can't lie to her. She'll probably think you're insane, and that I—"

"Made a big mistake in agreeing to marry me."

"That I'm taking terrible advantage of you," she corrected.

Gabe released a long breath. "Well, you're not. And I'll tell her so myself."

"I wonder..."

"What?"

"How she's going to feel about being a grand-mother."

Gabe couldn't stop himself. He went back to hunker down at her side. She looked so lost, so afraid.

"If it's your baby, Red, she'll love it," he said gently.

She reached out to him again, this time resting her hand at the back of his neck. The act was so warm, so easy, so intimate that Gabe's heart skipped a beat. It took every ounce of strength he had to merely smile at her, then stand away.

She trusted him, she relied on him. He couldn't afford to ruin it all with one foolish lapse.

"I have to go back to the station," he said. But he didn't move.

"I'll be all right," she tried to assure him. "Don't worry."

"I'll call later...to see how things are going."

"I'll be all right," she said again.

The telephone rang, causing both of them to jump. The answering machine kicked in and delivered the old recorded message. On the tape Gabe's voice told the caller to leave their name and a number where they could be reached if they wanted to be called back. The machine whirred and beeped, then a voice—that of Annabelle Scanlon, Tyler's Postmistress and undisputed maven of gossip—boomed into the room. "Gabe! Raine! I was away at a meeting all day and just heard the news. You could have knocked me over with a feather! I can't believe...! One of you give me a call just as soon as you can. I'm sure everyone in town would like to give you some kind of gift. But no one's sure what to get, what you might need. So give me a call and—'' The tape cut off.

Gabe and Raine looked at each other.

Neither said anything, but each knew what the other was thinking—thank heaven for answering machines!

A small smile pulled at the corner of Raine's mouth, to be answered by a similar twitch of Gabe's lips.

RAINE COULDN'T SETTLE at anything. Once again alone in the house, she wandered from room to room as dusk faded into night. She could only imagine what her mother must be thinking, must be feeling as she and George made their way back to Wisconsin.

The answering machine continued to record incoming calls. Most were from people curious about the marriage, but a few were from people asking assistance from Gabe. Diffident, needy-sounding people. One, an elderly man, asked if Gabe could repair a broken window. Another, a woman whose preteen son was causing her trouble, wanted Gabe to give him a good talking to. Another, an older woman with a cracking voice, requested that he come change a lightbulb in a ceiling fixture.

Raine paced about the house, yawning repeatedly in spite of her determination to resist the waves of sleepiness that had started to fell her at about this time each evening. It was one of the natural manifestations of her pregnancy, she'd read in the literature the New York doctor had given her. Understanding that helped, but it didn't make her happy about it. Particularly considering that she would soon have to face her mother. Nature won out, though, and before long she had stretched out on the couch and fallen into a deep, restorative sleep.

She had no idea what time it was when the doorbell rang, or even where she was. Nothing was as she remembered it. Then she realized that she was in Tyler, married to Gabe, and the person continuing to ring the doorbell was undoubtedly her mother, whom she would have to explain everything to.

She pushed the loose hair out of her face and sat up. The clock on the mantel read eleven-thirty.

"Just a second," she called through the door, after using her New York caution to check that it truly was her mother outside. She fumbled with the latch on her first try and had to try again.

The door swung open and light from the living room flooded the porch, allowing the two women to look at each other—mother and daughter, tension mirrored on each of their faces.

Marge had turned fifty on her last birthday, but because of the difficulties in her life, she'd frequently looked years older than her true age. Responsibility had been a heavy burden that dragged her down. Earlier in the year, though, she'd had her hair restyled and colored to a warmer shade of brown, her makeup had been updated, and in consultation with Nora Gates Forrester, owner of Gates Department Store, she had chosen a new wardrobe. She still looked like Marge, Raine's mother, but there was a new energy about her, a new confidence. Raine had received pages of her mother's quips and observations while the transformation took place. She'd also received a photograph of the finished product and had been amazed at the changes. But this was the first time she'd seen her mother in person.

Raine absorbed everything about her in the first few seconds. Marge, staring back at her, must have been equally quick in sensing the pain and confusion that held her daughter captive.

Marge stepped into the house, closed the door and extended her arms. Raine's response was instant. She slipped into her embrace, at once feeling welcomed and protected like the young child she longed to be. Gone was the strain that had lingered between them during the past seven years—the quiet disapproval, the corresponding resentment. The only thing that mattered was the love each felt for the other.

At that special moment nothing could hold back Raine's tears. "I'm sorry," she said after a time, sniffing and trying to smile. "I'm sorry you had to come back from your trip so early. I'm sorry I—"

Marge smoothed Raine's hair away from her face. "I told you," she said. "The trip wasn't all that wonderful. George and I were thinking of coming back early anyway."

"Not this early," Raine murmured.

Marge smiled slightly, worry and concern still evident in her brown eyes.

"Where is he?" Raine asked, straightening. She glanced belatedly past her mother, looking for George.

"At home. I thought it best if I came alone. Raine, will you please tell me what's going on?"

Raine turned partially away. "I told you. Gabe and I are married."

Marge caught her daughter's arm and brought her

to the couch. "Tell me everything," she com-
manded, sitting Raine down and taking a seat herself.

Raine's heart rate quickened. She didn't want to
do this. She didn't want to have to confess how stupid she'd been—to get pregnant, to think that Joel…
"I'm pregnant, Mom," she said tightly.

For a moment she wondered if Marge had heard.
Her mother was so quiet, so still. Raine chanced a
quick look, and from the expression on her mother's
face knew that she had.

"Is the baby Gabe's?" Marge asked at last.

"No," Raine admitted in a choked voice.

"Whose is it?" her mother asked.

"Someone—someone you don't know. A man
named Joel Hastings. He and I—"

"Why didn't *he* marry you?"

Raine looked down. "He wants me to have an
abortion. He…doesn't want children."

She sensed her mother's deep frown. Was she
thinking about the man she'd married, Raine's father,
who had walked out on them shortly after Raine was
born? Had he not wanted children, either? Or had the
added responsibility just become too much for him?

"I see," Marge said finally.

Raine was concerned with the way her mother was
holding herself, the tautness of her shoulders. Deep
regret again washed over her. She was bringing pain
to so many people, disrupting so many lives. Maybe
it would have been best for everyone if she'd just
done as Joel suggested. Not ask any questions. Not…
think.

She started to speak again, but her mother interrupted her. "Is that why you married Gabe? To give
the baby a name? Two mistakes don't make a right,

Lorraine. Gabe is too good a man to be trifled with, to be taken advantage of.''

"Mom, I'm not—''

"Or you could have had the baby on your own. Heaven knows things are a lot easier today than when I—'' She broke off.

"The same thing happened to you?'' Raine breathed.

"I was going to say, when I was a young woman. No, I was married to your father all right and proper, Raine. We waited until after the ceremony to make love for the first time…not that that did a lot of good. He certainly didn't stick around very long after you were born.''

"I thought about it,'' Raine replied tightly. "I thought about everything, even an abortion. But…would you really have wanted me to get rid of the baby? I never thought you, of all people…''

"I know how hard raising a child on your own can be. But no—'' Marge's expression softened "—I wouldn't want that.''

"I couldn't do it,'' Raine said miserably.

Her mother put an arm around her shoulders and pulled her close. "How did Gabe come into this?''

"There was a storm…you weren't home. I couldn't get into the house…and he found me.''

"He would.''

Raine closed her eyes. "I'm not sure I've done the right thing, Mom. He wanted to marry me when he found out. It was his idea! But—but right after the ceremony, I had second thoughts. Not for me, for him! It's not his problem that I'm pregnant, or that the man I—I thought loved me, didn't love me enough to—''

"Where's Gabe now? At work?"

Raine nodded.

"When did all this happen?" Marge asked.

"Yesterday. Reverend...I think her name is Reverend Sarah. Does that sound familiar?"

Marge nodded. "Sarah Kenton. She married you?"

Again Raine nodded.

"Didn't she ask any questions?"

"Why should she? I'm twenty-five and Gabe's twenty—"

"Twenty-nine, I know." Marge sighed. "I still come back to the question, why did you do it? You and Gabe...you're more like brother and sister than—"

"We still are!" Raine rushed to say. "We're not...the marriage isn't... We aren't... But we don't want anyone to know. To keep down the gossip. So that after, Gabe won't be hurt as badly."

"After?" Marge repeated.

"We don't plan for this to be forever. Just until after the baby's born and I can get my life back together. I don't have any money, Mom. Not enough to speak of. Or insurance. I'm just a week short of qualifying from last year. And the part I told you about—the job I just got? I couldn't keep it. It wouldn't be fair to the producers or the rest of the cast."

Marge shook her head slowly. "But to marry *Gabe!*"

"He's my best friend. We both understand the situation. Talk to him tomorrow, Mom. He'll tell you the same thing."

Marge closed her eyes and continued to shake her head.

Raine looked miserably down at her hands. So many wrong choices, so many wrong decisions. If only she could have the chance to make any one of them again...

"Mom?" she ventured softly.

Marge didn't seem to hear her.

"Mom?" Raine repeated. "Will you mind being a grandma?" The last word lingered in the room, echoing quietly, yet with enormous power.

Marge opened her eyes. "I'll love being a grandma," she said. Then she reached out again and gathered her daughter close to her heart.

CHAPTER SIX

GEORGE PHELPS SAT out on the back patio "smoking" his empty pipe. Gabe saw him as he cut across his driveway, on his way to his front door.

When George waved, Gabe didn't have any option but to change direction and say hello. Technically, the man was now his father-in-law.

"So, Doc," he said, claiming a self-assurance he didn't fully feel, "you're back."

George got up with slow deliberation and walked to the hedge. Tall and fit and in his late fifties, he had the distinguished air of a person accustomed to authority and respect. Born into one of the prominent families of Tyler, he had made his biggest contribution to the community while serving long years as chief of staff at Tyler General Hospital. Now, after having chosen early retirement from day-to-day practice, he saw only the occasional patient.

"I hear congratulations are in order," George said.

It was bad enough that the unexpected marriage had thrown Marge into a tizzy, which directly affected George, but the vacation he'd probably been enjoying had been canceled as well. Gabe wasn't sure how the older man would react. "Yes, well..." he hedged.

"Marge also told me about the baby...about what you've done for Raine. Don't worry," George assured Gabe quickly as he started to frown. "I won't tell anyone. I took an oath to keep my mouth shut a long time ago, and I also promised Marge. Now, I'll just say this once and I won't say it again…but it's something I think needs to be said. I've seen a lot during my years practicing medicine in this town. People sometimes think that because we live in a small place we're insulated from the normal troubles of life. That we inhabit some kind of perfect world. Those people are stupid. The things I've seen people do here, to themselves and to others…" He shook his graying head. "But every once in a while you see some good things happen, too. And good people. You're one of those good people, Gabe. No—" he raised his hand to stop Gabe from protesting "—let me finish. I've been watching you for a long time. Watching how you care about people, the big and little things you do for them. And I'm not talking about your job. This is after hours, on your own time. Well, now you're bringing it home to us. You're doing something for Raine, which means you're doing some-thing for Marge, which means you're doing something for me. And I'm not going to let the moment pass without acknowledging it. I'd like to shake your hand, son."

Gabe stared at the proffered hand. Dr. George Phelps had always been a distant figure during Gabe's growing years. The older man had been busy at the hospital and with his duties on the board of directors at Worthington House, not to mention other various services to Tyler. After he'd married Marge and moved next door, he'd still seemed somewhat distant. Now he wanted to shake Gabe's hand…because Gabe had done what he'd wanted to do for many years—marry Raine.

Feeling something of a fraud, Gabe clasped the hand extended to him. George's handshake was firm, confident. He tried to equal it.

"Welcome to the family," George said mildly.

"Thanks, Doc," Gabe murmured. Then he glanced back over his shoulder toward his house.

George noticed. "Don't let me keep you," he said. "I know you're just getting off duty, and I remember what that was like." He then jammed the pipe stem back in his mouth and retraced his steps to the chair.

Gabe completed his shortcut across the front yard and let himself into the house. Again, as he'd found last evening, everything was quiet. But unlike the evening before, Raine was not sitting curled on the edge of the couch.

She'd seen her mother, talked with her. How had she come through it? Was she all right?

Gabe tiptoed down the hall, unwilling to wake her if she was asleep. The door to her room was ajar. He hesitated, then peeked inside.

His father's room smelled of her delicate perfume. Her robe was draped over the back of the easy chair. She was in his father's bed, under the cover, very still, her bright, copper-colored hair spread out on the white pillow like a halo.

Gabe stared at her, unable to move…because if he moved, it would be toward her, not away.

She stirred and he instinctively tried to fade back into the hall, but the heel of his shoe thumped against the doorjamb and she sat up at the sound.

She wore a white cotton nightgown instead of the pink pajamas. The gown was sleeveless, with a scoop neck that exposed a teasing glimpse of cleavage. Gabe had to forcefully lift his gaze.

"Gabe?" she questioned, blinking.

"Sorry I woke you," he murmured. "I was just…checking. I saw the doc just now and he said—"

"They're back, yes." Raine yawned and stretched prettily, like a cat. Using both hands, she threaded her fingers through her hair to push it away from her face.

She was so beautiful she might have been a painting come to life. Her bright hair, her contrasting pale skin, her face and body so perfectly formed… The mere sight of her made Gabe physically ache.

"Mom came over last night," she said. Then her arms slowly fell. "Gabe? Are you all right? You look—"

Gabe recovered quickly. "I'm fine, just tired. We had a couple of calls during the night—one was particularly bad. A wreck on the highway between a truck and a car. I'm going to have to hit the sack for a couple of hours this morning to catch up on my sleep."

"I thought I heard a siren earlier."

"That must have been the call to Gunther and Fourth Street." He named a location a few blocks away.

"Was it serious?"

Gabe chuckled and rubbed his cheek. "Just someone making a late-night snack. The man fell asleep at the table and smoke filled the house. The smoke alarm went off and a neighbor called us in. The man was pretty embarrassed when we rolled up."

"I can imagine."

Gabe leaned against the doorjamb. "What did your mom have to say?"

"A lot of stuff. Mostly what I told you she'd say. She wants to talk to you, too."

"It wouldn't be the first time," Gabe murmured. "She used to give me almost as many lectures as my dad did."

Raine smiled in remembrance.

Gabe continued to look at her, not realizing that time was passing.

She gave a small laugh. "You're going to be asleep on your feet if you don't lie down soon."

Gabe was tired; he hadn't lied about that. But at the moment, sleep was the farthest thing from his mind. Still, he pushed away from the jamb and murmured, "You're probably right. Don't let me sleep past ten-thirty, all right? That is, if you're up by then."

"I'll be up," she assured him. "Mom said she'd be over around eleven."

Gabe nodded and turned away.

SECONDS LATER the shower switched on and a short time after that switched off. Next came the sound of Gabe's footsteps as he made his way down the hall and turned into the bedroom directly opposite his father's. Raine snuggled luxuriously under the cover. She was glad to hear the soft sounds of his presence. Yesterday had been a very long and lonely day.

She stayed in bed for another half hour, trying to give Gabe enough time to fall asleep. Once up, she puttered quietly about the house—reading the local newspaper, the *Citizen,* which Gabe had brought inside, washing the few dishes she had used the day before and feeding Frederica. The little fish sucked the flakes into her mouth before most had time to settle on the bright blue rocks lining the bottom of the bowl.

Raine was sitting at the kitchen table, nursing a second cup of tea and leafing through a magazine, when Gabe stirred back to life and came into the room. He yawned as he claimed the chair opposite her.

"Good morning." She smiled. "You look all ready to take on the world."

His reply was something between a grunt and a groan, which quickly evolved into another yawn. "Yesterday felt like two days put together."

"I heard you gave a fire-safety talk to a preschool class."

"From Britt? Yeah. But talking to kids isn't bad. Not when you know you might be saving a life. The little ones need to learn what a fire fighter in full gear looks like. Kids have died because they get scared when they see us at a fire and hide. They think we're monsters or something. They need to see that underneath our suit and breathing equipment we're a person just like Mommy or Daddy." He smiled dryly. "They do ask a lot of questions, though."

"You had some calls yesterday," she informed him.

"I'll bet."

Raine shook her head. "No, I mean real calls. From people you'll probably want to call back."

He started to get up.

"You're going to call them back now?" she asked, surprised.

"Something wrong with that?" His gaze was quizzical.

"No. Just…don't you want some coffee or something to eat first?" Joel never called anyone back right away, not even when he had the time. *They'll call again if they're serious,* he used to tell her. And he especially didn't like to be disturbed in the morning, by her or anyone else, until he'd absorbed at least two cups of coffee.

"Not now," Gabe said easily. "It can wait."

He disappeared into the living room, where she soon heard him dialing a number.

She finished her tea, then got up to make his coffee. He'd done so many nice things for her, trying to cheer her up. It was the least she could do to try to repay his thoughtfulness.

"Some of my regulars," Gabe said when he came back a short time later. He sniffed the air and made a pleased sound. "Mmm, great! I'm ready for a cup now."

"Sit down and I'll pour," she volunteered.

Gabe smiled up at her as she filled his cup—that sweet Gabe smile that meant so much to her. She'd been on the receiving end of it so often over the years.

"You'll spoil me," he said.

"Maybe you need a little spoiling. From what I've seen so far, you don't get very much."

"Be careful," he teased. "You might make me think you care."

Raine paused in the act of sitting down again, and Gabe, seeing her reaction, suddenly found something to do with his shoelace. It was one of those moments when someone said something that came a little too close to an unspoken truth. But of course she cared for him! she asserted to herself. He was her friend!

Raine cleared throat. "Of course I care," she said firmly.

Double taps—the private signal—sounded on the kitchen door. Both of them looked up and into each other's eyes. The discomfort that had momentarily flared between them might never have been.

The taps sounded again, followed by Marge calling, "Raine? Gabe? Are you there?"

Raine got up to let her mother inside.

Marge hugged them both before joining them at the table. She refused their offer of something to drink. Instead, she folded her hands in front of her and said seriously, "I think this is a very foolish thing you've done. It didn't have to be this way. Not in this day and age. Unmarried women are having babies and raising them alone all the time...not that I think that's the best way, from my own experience. But that's neither here nor there. It's done. You're married. And the people of Tyler know about it. So the only thing we can do—George and I—is to support you all the way. If you want me to, I'll pretend that I knew about it all the time. That I knew you planned to get married, but not when. That the whim struck you and you did it and I don't mind in the least." She turned to Gabe. "It won't be a lie that I think of you as a son, Gabe, because I do. Have you told your father yet?"

Gabe shook his head. "Not yet. We thought we'd give him a little more time on his vacation. We didn't really want to tell you...but you called and talked to Raine."

Marge said, "One of the best things I ever did was

to forget to leave that key behind. It really would have looked strange for George and me to stay in the dark. I know how the gossips think around here. Someone would have called and given me the news—several of my waitresses had the number— and I'm not as good an actress as you are, Raine. I wouldn't have fooled anyone on the spur of the moment.'' Marge stood up. ''Well, that's about it, I guess. This isn't going to be easy, particularly when Raine's pregnancy starts to show. The tongues will wag again. But words can't hurt anybody. You just have to keep your head up and keep going.''

''I'm glad you're not angry, Marge,'' Gabe said quietly.

She smiled. ''Shocked was more like it. But now that's wearing off. It'll wear off with the town, too…eventually.''

Gabe and Raine remained at the table after Marge left, each lost in thought. Then Raine stood up and reached for his cup. ''Let me heat this,'' she said. ''It's probably cold by now.''

''It's fine,'' Gabe replied, intercepting her.

Her fingers were beneath his, and she twisted her hand until they were entwined. ''Have you come to regret what you did, Gabe?'' she asked quietly. ''Yesterday must have been a nightmare for you…and now this. Mom's a strong person. She's had to be. But sometimes she can come down a little hard.''

''Your mother is one of the finest people I know.''

Raine sighed and nodded in agreement, once again ridiculously near to tears. She hated the way her emotions were so close to the surface—another side effect of the pregnancy, she'd read. It wasn't like her to cry or to be so easily upset. Yet even without her spiking hormones, the past few months had not been easy. More than once she'd found herself stinging from something Joel had said or done. He wasn't an easy person to live with. He was spoiled, he was difficult...but because he was so brilliant, so arresting and creative, she'd let herself be swept along on the currents of his desires. What would her mother think of Joel? she wondered. And, equally, what would Joel have thought of her mother?

"Hey, Red," Gabe said softly, breaking into her musings. "How'd you like to take a little walk? One of those calls earlier was from a lady in distress. Remember Mrs. Franklin from elementary school? The ceiling light is out in her kitchen and I told her I'd be over soon to change it. Want to come along?"

"Mrs. Franklin?" Raine echoed.

He nodded. "She's ninety-two now, still lives at home, does almost everything for herself, but she can't climb a ladder. Her grandchildren would like her to move into Worthington House, but she refuses. Not as long as she can still 'percolate,' as she puts it."

"Mrs. Franklin! She was my teacher in second grade!"

"Mine, too. She's still pretty much the same. Whenever I do anything for her, I have to do it right. 'A job is not worth doing if it's not done properly, Gabriel.'" He chuckled at his mimicry of Mrs. Franklin's prim mannerisms.

"I'd love to see her," Raine said.

"Then let's do it."

Gabe pulled her from her chair.

IT FELT ODD to Raine to be out and about in Tyler. In the past, during her short return trips to the town of her birth, she'd stayed at her mother's house and rarely left except for quick trips to the Diner or for a special meal at Timberlake Lodge. She'd never taken the time to explore the streets she'd known as a child and a teenager. Now it was with a sense of enjoyment that she recognized houses and noticed small changes.

"Oh, look! Old Mrs. Atkins's place!" she exclaimed as they passed in front of a tall Victorian that once had belonged to Rose Atkins, one of Tyler's more colorful characters. Before her death a few years earlier, the elderly woman had been regularly seen riding around on her three-wheel bike, running errands and transporting herself to her quilting-circle meetings. "Mom wrote about what Susannah and Joe were doing with the place. Granny Rose's...what a wonderful name for a bed-and-breakfast! Mrs. Atkins would be pleased."

The front door opened and a strikingly pretty young woman with dark hair flowing loosely over her shoulders came out on the porch to shake a small rug. She went back inside without noticing them.

"Who was that?" Raine asked.

"Gina Santori," Gabe said.

Raine's eyebrows lifted. "Joe's daughter? The last time I saw her she was what—twelve? Now she's—"

"Seven years makes a lot of difference. Particularly with young girls."

Raine sent him a speculative look. "She certainly has grown up. You've, ah, noticed?"

Gabe's lips twitched. "I'm a married man, remember?"

"Not for long."

"Stop trying to matchmake."

"I'm just pointing out that she's a very pretty young woman."

"I have eyes."

"Oh, well, excuse me." Raine grinned. "Next time I won't say anything."

"Good." A moment passed. "What are you laughing at?" he demanded, looking at her sideways.

"Oh, nothing…male sensitivity, I guess. Does Mrs. Franklin live around here? I don't remember ever being at her house before."

"That's her place over there." Gabe pointed to the gracefully aging two-story Victorian up the street. It was the second house from the corner and faced the elementary school.

"I never realized she lived that close to the school," Raine commented. "But then in second grade I never really gave much thought to the fact that my teacher 'lived' anywhere. If I'd been asked, I'd probably have said that she lived at the school!"

Gabe chuckled. "Which was probably the way she preferred it—keeping all the kids in the dark in order to preserve her sanity."

He motioned for Raine to precede him onto the narrow porch, where without hesitation he knocked on one of the sturdy double doors. Both were inset with an oval of thick glass and covered on the inside by delicate lace sheers.

It took a few moments before a fragile hand pulled aside a portion of the lace, then released it to open one of the doors.

Mrs. Franklin looked much as Raine remembered her—small and delicately made, yet with an innate dignity that time had not dulled. She'd always seemed old to Raine, with her silver hair and parchmentlike skin. If she was ninety-two now, she had to have been in her mid-seventies when Raine was in second grade. She'd retired the next year.

"Gabriel!" The old woman greeted him warmly, her crackly voice the same one Raine had heard on the answering machine the day before.

"Hello, Beth," he responded, a special warmth entering his tone. His use of their stern teacher's first name widened Raine's eyes. "I've brought along someone you might like to see again. Do you remember Lorraine Peterson?"

Raine felt the old woman's eyes turn on her and narrow. "Aren't you supposed to be in New York?" Beth Franklin demanded.

"I've moved back, Mrs. Franklin. How are you?" Raine asked.

"As well as can be expected, I suppose." She turned to Gabe as she saw them inside. "Gabriel, now I've had a second bulb burn out. Would you mind replacing it as well? One is in the kitchen and the other in the pantry."

Stepping into Beth Franklin's house was like entering another age. Raine's eyes widened even more as she followed the others into the living room, which was decorated in the Victorian style with mounds of clutter. Every available surface was taken up with old and beautiful keepsakes and trinkets. Heavy, dark curtains on the high windows blotted out the sunlight, while tall floor lamps—some with shades edged in fringe, some without—pooled yellowish light on the period furniture and muted, jewel-patterned rugs.

"We'll wait here for you to finish, Gabriel. Then, if you like, you may bring the lemonade from the refrigerator and the tray I've already prepared and have waiting on the counter."

"Certainly," Gabe replied, and after giving Raine a surreptitious wink, he disappeared through a doorway that led to the rear of the house.

"Sit down, Lorraine," Beth Franklin said, before she slowly and carefully settled herself in a chair.

Raine sat, more than a trifle uncomfortably, in another chair. Mrs. Franklin had been a stern taskmaster, even to children of seven or eight. She'd taught by the old style—a child was to be heard only when given permission. Homework had to be done and handed in before class began, and frequent tests were the only way to measure just how much the student had learned. To say that Raine had learned a great deal more in second grade than she did in some of her later grades was wholly accurate. Mrs. Franklin had expected great effort from her pupils and accepted nothing less. Raine had never felt that she measured up, and now, even though she was grown, she still felt the same way.

"Tell me about yourself," her old teacher instructed. "I've heard a little from time to time, but not enough. You sing and dance on the stage?"

"Yes, ma'am."

"Are you good at it?"

"I think so."

"And act? I've heard that, too."

Raine smiled tightly. Mrs. Franklin would no doubt consider her choice of career a terrible waste.

But Beth Franklin leaned forward and, before Raine could answer, confided, "This is going to shock you. A long time ago I would have given everything I had to be able to do that." The older woman enjoyed Raine's start of surprise. "I would," she repeated. "I even considered going to Chicago to work at a speakeasy. I had a fairly good voice and I thought someone might see me and help me get on the stage. But Father discovered my plans and that was the end of that. I ended up getting married and then teaching."

"I never…"

"I know. You thought I was an old fuddy-duddy, as did everyone else."

Raine truly didn't know what to say.

Beth Franklin began singing a song from the twenties, one of the many silly, happy little songs that were a perfect reflection of the time. Obviously her voice wasn't as good as it used to be, but there were enough flashes of sweetness and purity to show that she once did have talent.

"My husband didn't think singing was seemly for someone in my position, so I didn't sing anymore."

"How sad," Raine murmured.

"For him, yes. He wasn't a very happy man. I couldn't make him happy. I tried," she said with a sigh, "but it didn't work."

Raine stretched her neck, hoping to catch sight of Gabe. She was starting to gain the impression that Mrs. Franklin's mind was occasionally a little dreamy. She was saying things that the old Mrs. Franklin would never have said.

Gabe came back into the room at that moment, and Raine smiled at him in relief.

"Job's all done, Beth," he said as he settled the lemonade tray on the low table in front of the couch. "Both lightbulbs are replaced. Would you like me to serve us?"

"That would be wonderful, Gabriel."

Gabe carefully filled the glasses and handed them around. "Cookie?" he offered next.

Raine shook her head, but Mrs. Franklin took one. "I always have loved lemonade," the older woman reflected, looking at her glass as Gabe took a seat on the couch. "I think I like it because I remember it being such a treat when I was a child. I was born in Alabama, you know. Mobile. My family didn't move to Wisconsin until I was nearly ten. I don't sound like it, do I? My Southern accent is completely gone. My father said we had to fit in, so he used to slap our hands with a switch every time we slipped and said something the wrong way. The backs of my hands were red far more often than my sister's, but I eventually learned."

Raine took a sip of lemonade, then had to stifle a grimace. The mixture was very strong and very sour.

With her lips puckering, she looked desperately at Gabe and saw his amusement. He took a bite of cookie, but didn't touch his drink. "Are you sure you haven't changed your mind, Raine?" he asked, once again offering her the plate of cookies.

Raine took one and ate it in self-defense. The cookie, a store-bought macaroon, helped mitigate the sour taste.

"Thanks," she murmured when she could.

Gabe turned to Mrs. Franklin. "Beth, has your grandson come over to take those old newspapers and magazines away yet?"

"I've asked him to, but he hasn't…not yet."

"I've told you I'd be glad to do it."

The old woman shook her head. "No. That wouldn't be fair. Bobby said he'll come do it and he will."

"Maybe he's too busy right now."

"Well, he is, but he told me he'd be around just as soon as he could find the time."

"Would you like me to talk to him?" Gabe volunteered.

"No. I can manage."

"It's not a good idea to have that much old paper lying around. Especially on a back porch. It could catch fire."

Beth's laugh was girlish. "No, it won't. You're just saying that."

"No, I'm not." Gabe was firm but patient.

"Did I ever show you the school papers I kept? They're upstairs. Would you like to see?"

Gabe shook his head. "No, Beth. Not now. Raine and I have to leave. We have a couple more errands to do."

Without argument, Mrs. Franklin stood up. Almost as if it were a mantle, she resumed her poised and proper pose. "Well, I'm very glad that you could come have lemonade with me, and also that you brought Lorraine. We've had a very nice chat. You both must come again soon."

"We will, Beth," Gabe promised.

"We will," Raine echoed.

Mrs. Franklin saw them to the door, then waved them on their way.

Raine didn't say anything until they were halfway

down the path to the sidewalk. "Why didn't you tell me?" she whispered.

"Because some days she's fine and some days she's not. This was a not."

"At least about the lemonade!" she insisted.

He grinned. "That's hit-and-miss, too. Sometimes it's just fine."

"She's gone a little batty, hasn't she?"

"Only a little. She's a sweet old thing."

"Now I understand why her grandchildren want her in Worthington House. How can she take care of herself?"

"Her grandchildren want her in Worthington House so they can have her house. They want to sell off all the furnishings, get rid of her keepsakes—"

Raine was dismayed. "You know this for a fact?"

"Bobby told me straight out."

"But is she okay on her own like that?"

"Probably, for a little while longer. She keeps the place as neat as a pin. She's always cleaning. If she's forced to leave too soon..."

Raine didn't prompt him to finish. The point of his conjecture was readily apparent. If their old teacher was made to give up everything she loved, she might decide, consciously or unconsciously, to give up on life as well.

"Maybe I'll go back to visit with her from time to time," Raine murmured.

"Good idea," Gabe exclaimed approvingly.

Raine flashed him a curious look. Had that been his aim all along?

CHAPTER SEVEN

RAINE ENDED UP tagging along with Gabe as he made his two remaining calls. He measured the windowpane that needed to be replaced at Mr. Foster's house, assuring the elderly gentleman that he would return later that afternoon to finish the job. Then they stopped by Ann Tully's house, where Gabe listened to a detailed account of her twelve-year-old son's latest misadventures.

"Cory listens to you, Gabe," Ann Tully said. "You're the only adult who can get through to him. I certainly can't! I'm sorry he left with his friends when he wasn't supposed to. You will come again, won't you? I realize this is a bad time for you and all, but..."

The look the pretty brunette sent Raine told Raine much more than the woman might have liked. It was obvious that, until hearing the news about Gabe's unexpected marriage, the woman had hoped his involvement with her family would go far deeper than merely acting as counselor to her troubled son. Whether Gabe knew that or not was hard for Raine to tell. His manner was easygoing and friendly, but that was the way he behaved toward most people.

"Sure, I'll come back," Gabe said.

"I hate to intrude...."

Gabe draped an arm around Raine's shoulders and

pulled her close. "Raine won't mind, will you?" he prompted.

"Of course not," Raine murmured.

He gave her a lopsided smile before releasing her. "Just give me a call when Cory shows up again. If I'm not at home, Raine will know where to find me."

Back on the sidewalk, Raine was quiet. After leaving Mr. Foster's house, Gabe had told her the old man was alone in the world and often used needed repairs as an excuse to talk to someone. When she'd asked if he thought Mr. Foster had broken his own window, Gabe had shrugged.

"What's the story here?" she prompted.

"Ann's had a tough time of it lately. She and her husband were divorced last year, then the fire shut down the F and M. She worked on the assembly line and her ex worked in shipping. He took off shortly after that and hasn't been heard from since. Now she's having to accept financial assistance, and Cory's causing all kinds of trouble. Not a good situation."

"She said he listens to you."

Gabe shrugged again. "For ten minutes maybe."

Raine fell back into silence.

Throughout their walk in the neighborhood the streets had been quiet. The nearer they drew to the center of town, though, activity began to pick up, and Raine's steps lagged.

Noticing, Gabe asked, "What's up?"

Raine stopped walking all together. "I want to go home now, Gabe. I've enjoyed getting out and meeting a few people, but I'm not ready yet to meet more."

The town square had always been the nerve center

of Tyler, with people bustling in and out of shops and offices and strolling in the grassy park. So far Gabe and she had escaped notice. If they continued on, that wouldn't last.

"You're going to have to face people sooner or later," Gabe said.

"I know." She turned to retrace her steps.

"They're basically good people," Gabe said, catching up.

"I'm not as sure of that as you are."

"The folks we visited this morning didn't attack you."

"No, but then, they're not exactly in tip-top form, are they?"

"Whenever you're ready, let me know."

Raine glanced at him. His reply had held a prickly edge that he had never used with her before.

"You think I'm being a coward, don't you?" she retorted, smarting. "That I'm too involved in my own problems. That's what this morning was all about, wasn't it? Introduce me to people who are coping with difficulties far greater than my own, so I'll feel guilty!"

"I never wanted to make you feel guilty."

"But a little healthy contrition would do me a world of good, wouldn't it?" she challenged. "I did something stupid, now I have to pay!"

Gabe's jaw tightened. "You're free to leave any time you like, Raine. I won't keep you here."

Tears pricked at her eyes. She hadn't meant to get into an argument. Not with Gabe. She lengthened her stride. Their homes were just ahead.

"I wanted to get you out of the house, that's all," Gabe explained tightly.

Just then brakes screeched and the door of a car flew open, disgorging Annabelle Scanlon.

"Oh, I'm so happy to see you!" the woman exclaimed, hurrying over to greet them. "Did you get my message? I left several, but you must have...well, never mind. Now it doesn't matter, because I can pass on my good wishes in person!" She attached herself to Gabe, then turned with the same intent toward Raine. But Gabe stepped in front of the woman, blocking her path.

"Annabelle," he murmured, "do you think we could we do this another time? Raine isn't feeling very well at the moment."

Annabelle blinked, her short, pudgy body temporarily arrested. "Not feeling well?" she repeated. She tried to peer around Gabe, but he moved again, continuing to obstruct her view. "Yes," he said. "It was probably something she ate."

Annabelle smiled slyly. "Or something else *very* natural. When is the blessed event going to be, Gabe? There's no use pretending. Everyone will know for sure soon enough." She touched his arm to keep him in place and tried for a third time to see around him. "Raine?" she called. "When people ask what kind of wedding present you might like, do you want me to tell some of them to give you baby things?"

Raine witnessed the not-so-subtle struggle taking place between Gabe and Annabelle, and felt it ridiculous to continue hiding. She gathered a measure of control and stepped forward.

"Annabelle," she said, greeting the older woman warmly.

Gabe stopped defending Raine, and the postmistress lurched forward to give her a quick hug.

"You're absolutely blooming!" Annabelle decreed, her eyes taking in every element of Raine's appearance. "A new marriage, a new baby! How wonderful for you!"

Raine slipped her arm through Gabe's and rested her head on his shoulder. "Yes, isn't it?" she breathed dreamily.

"No one suspected a thing," Annabelle continued. "You two certainly played your cards close to your chests. But tell me, when is the baby due?"

"The middle of November," Raine replied, forcing a smile.

"November," Annabelle repeated. It was apparent she was ticking back the months in her mind. "So you're going on three months!" She turned to Gabe. "Ahh…that vacation you took last February! Gabe, you sly dog!"

"You must have been an excellent math student, Annabelle," he said mildly.

"Why, yes," she responded, highly pleased at what she considered a compliment. "As a matter of fact, I was."

"Annabelle, why don't you tell people not to bother with gifts at all?" Raine suggested. "Gabe and I want things to be low-key. We don't want a fuss."

"It wouldn't be a fuss! But if that's what you want…"

"It is. Now, if you don't mind, I would like to rest."

"Oh, of course. Of course. This is a time when you really must take good care of yourself. Gabe, you remember how hard Cece's pregnancy was." She named her daughter, who was married to Jeff

Baron, the present chief of staff at the hospital. "But then she was carrying twins. Both girls, Raine. Did your mother tell you?"

"I think they'd already been born the last time I visited Tyler."

"They're three now. Would you like to see some pictures?" She started to open her purse.

"Another time, Annabelle?" Gabe suggested, repeating his original request.

The postmistress rolled her eyes heavenward. "Oh, my, yes. I'm becoming so forgetful I'd lose my head if it wasn't attached. You go lie down, Raine, and I'll show you my pictures another time. Better yet, we can go over to Cece and Jeff's and you can see the girls yourself. They're such adorable little angels!"

When Annabelle was once again in her car, she waggled her fingers before starting the engine.

Raine and Gabe remained as they were—arms entwined, her head tipped against his shoulder.

"You deserve an Oscar," he murmured.

"Broadway performers receive a Tony," she returned.

"Whatever."

As Annabelle drove away, Raine closed her eyes. The second news bulletin would hit the Tyler airwaves as soon as the postmistress could get to a telephone. Up until that moment her pregnancy had just been speculation; now it was fact. From Raine's own lips.

"I'm sorry I was upset earlier," she apologized, tightening her grip on Gabe's arm and leaning even closer. "I wasn't angry with you. It was just... everything."

Gabe ruffled her hair. "All's forgiven, Red," he said. His reply had been easy, yet there was an unusual huskiness that caught Raine's notice.

For a moment she wondered what had happened to stir his emotions, but she dismissed further inquiry when she couldn't come up with an adequate answer.

GABE WENT TO WORK the next day, mindful that his marriage would continue to be the prime topic of conversation. His expectation was met first thing when he found a baby's rattle hanging from a blue ribbon on the handle of his locker.

"You're a fast worker, Gabe," one of his co-workers teased. "Sure don't mess around!" another one called.

"You trying to set a record?" a third demanded.

Gabe was heckled good-naturedly all around. Still, he could sense his colleagues' puzzlement and the numerous burning questions that hovered just beneath the surface.

Several times during the hours that followed he came upon small groups talking: Maureen and Bill, David and Bill, Maureen and David and Lynn, the station secretary. Each time they would grow quiet as soon as they saw him, a red flag that they'd been talking about him and Raine.

Gabe tried to ignore it, to let them hash it all out. They would anyway. But once, undetected, he got a little too close and overheard part of an exchange:

"Well, I for one don't believe the baby's his. How come we never heard him say anything about her? Wouldn't you think he'd have said *something?*"

"Gabe's pretty closemouthed about things like that."

"Not that quiet. It's unnatural!"

"Well, whose do you think it is?"

"Hell, I don't know! One of those fancy men she ran around with in New York. She gets herself knocked up, then comes running home, and guess who she asks for help?"

There was a pause, then, "Gabe's not that stupid."

"Why not? He's always doing things for people."

"But not that!"

"That's what I'm hearing people say."

"Who? Who says it?"

"Patricia Sikes."

There was a feminine snort of disbelief. "You believe *her?*"

"She and Raine are pretty close."

"I don't remember it that way. When we were in school together they weren't all that—"

The alarm bell went off and everyone scattered, racing to get into their gear and to jump on the fire truck.

As Gabe took a seat just behind the driver, David McGregor, he longed to underscore what Maureen had just said. Patricia Sikes was no friend of Raine's. She'd always been jealous, envying Raine her looks, her talent and her drive, and you could believe very little of what she might have to say about her. But in this instance, Patricia was unknowingly right. And if Gabe said anything to refute it, he might end up only making matters worse. There were times, his father had once told him, when the best denial was complete silence. As hard as it was for Gabe to keep quiet, he had to concede that this was one of those times.

THE TELEPHONE RANG repeatedly again the next morning, and to escape it, Raine crossed the yard to her mother's house. Only Marge wasn't home, George explained upon answering her knock. She'd gone to the diner.

Raine stood restlessly on the patio step. She had expected her mother to be there.

George pushed the door open farther. "Would you like to come inside anyway? I know I'm second best, but…" He smiled. "Come on. She said she wasn't going to be long."

Raine shrugged and stepped inside. George Phelps was legally her stepfather, but she didn't feel close to him. He'd always been a shadowy figure in her memory—a successful physician married to someone else, living in one of the huge old mansions on Elm Street, where most of the crème de la crème of Tyler society had their homes.

"Of course, you know her," George continued, motioning Raine toward the cozy living room. "She could easily get involved in something and take half the day. I finally convinced her to ease up a bit, like me, but she can't seem to stay away from that place for more than a couple of days. She's always stopping in, just to see how things are going. That diner's in her blood. It's like her second child."

"I know," Raine murmured, perching on the edge of the sofa.

George stood across from her. In his late fifties, with a full head of graying hair and a nice, fatherly smile, he was a little less distinguished-looking now than she remembered him in years past. Today he was dressed in a pair of comfortable-looking khaki slacks and a softly rumpled shirt.

"Would you like something to drink?" he asked. "Some milk? Some orange juice?"

Her glance traveled to the easy chair that he'd recently left. The newspaper was lying open on one of the arms, and a partial glass of orange juice waited on the narrow table abutting it, along with his trademark empty pipe.

"Orange juice would be nice," she agreed.

His smile broadened. "Good for you," he said.

She heard the refrigerator door open and close and soon he was back, passing her her drink.

As he resettled in the easy chair, Raine sat back, trying to relax. She didn't quite know what to say to him. Always before, her mother had been present to smooth over any awkward moments between her new husband and her daughter. This was the first time they'd truly been alone.

"I suppose I should be glad I could persuade her to leave it at all," George continued, shaking his head. "If it weren't for Susie Mack, I don't think Marge would ever have agreed. She'd still be going in early every morning and staying late at night."

"Susie's who she finally settled on?"

"Been with her the longest. Marge says she's always been dead reliable as a waitress. Getting the manager's job came at a good time for Susie. Her husband worked at the F and M."

"That's really affected a lot of people, hasn't it?"

George frowned. "I just wish the business would get going again, so people could go back to work. Roger was involved—did you know that? Has anyone told you? He saw the explosion when he was out on a late night call. He hurried over, helped the night watchman—saved his life, actually. Then he called in to report the fire on his cellular phone.''

''I didn't know,'' Raine said. Roger was George's only son. For a time, five or six years earlier, he'd attended medical school in New York City, and while he was there, he and Raine had gotten together for lunch on a regular basis—two expatriates from Tyler comparing notes about their lives in the big city. Then had come the news of the trouble in his parents' marriage, coupled with the courtship of Marge and George and all the attendant stickiness around the separation and divorce. The upheaval hadn't been easy for either Roger or Raine. And in the end— amazingly!—they'd found themselves to be stepbrother and stepsister.

George nodded proudly. ''Well, he did.''

''How is he? It's been… We used to see each other all the time, but since he left New York—''

''He's doing fine, just fine.''

Raine glanced at George carefully. ''His, ah, veterinary practice is doing well?'' At one time George had been stubbornly determined that Roger should follow in his footsteps as a physician. An ''M.D.'' *would* be added to his name, period. No question. Raine had been amazed when Roger informed her at their last lunch together that he'd decided to leave medical school. She'd been even more amazed when, sometime later, she'd learned from her mother that he'd announced his intention to care for animals.

''Seems to be,'' George said. ''I heard from him last night. He told me to tell you he'd be calling soon.''

Raine couldn't prevent a smile. Roger definitely had a way about him. He covered a very tender heart with a great sense of humor. He never seemed to take anything too seriously—himself or most situations.

"And Melissa?" Raine prompted. Roger's older sister was Gabe's age. Unlike Roger, she'd always seemed highly aware of her family's place in Tyler society. She had a little too much of her mother in her, Marge had once said—the only time in Raine's memory her mother had commented negatively on anyone in the Phelps family.

"She's fine, too...I think," George said. "We're not exactly on the best of terms at the moment," he confessed. "She and her mother...live close to each other in Chicago."

"Do you get to see her children?" she asked softly, responding to the sadness she heard in his voice.

"No."

Raine fell silent. There were some in Tyler, she'd been told, who blamed Marge for the breakup of the Phelpses' marriage. But Raine knew her mother better than that. Her mother wasn't a home wrecker, and George, from everything she knew about him wasn't some kind of reckless lothario. If the marriage disintegrated, it had done so before Marge and George came together. Mary probably didn't see it that way, though, and neither, it seemed, did Melissa.

George motioned to her untouched glass. "Would you rather have something else?" he asked.

Raine had forgotten the orange juice. "No," she said and took a sip.

George watched her. "You don't have to drink it if you don't want to," he said.

"It's good for me," Raine answered.

"And the baby."

Raine's fingers tightened on the glass. "Yes."

"You're what—eleven to twelve weeks?"

Raine nodded.

"You've been examined by a physician?"

Again Raine nodded.

"In Tyler?" George persisted.

Raine shrugged. "Not here. Not yet."

"Hank Merton's one of the best obstetricians in the state."

"I know. I'm going to call him."

"What about a pediatrician?"

"I haven't thought about that yet. It seems so…"

"It's never too soon to start lining things up." He paused. "There's a new one in town. Close by, actually…just the other side of Mrs. Johnson's, in that big old Victorian. He came to claim his inheritance from his grandmother. Ruffled some feathers when he wanted to convert the bottom floor for his medical practice, but he's doing it anyway. He has impeccable credentials, excellent training and a lot of experience. Name's Paul Chambers. Maybe one day you should drop by and talk with him. I'll go with you, if you like, to introduce you."

Raine was having a hard enough time reconciling herself to the fact of her pregnancy and subsequent marriage. To take the next step—to actually make firm plans for what would happen after the birth— was more than she could handle at the moment. "No, I'll—I…" she faltered to a stop.

George's face softened. "I apologize," he said gruffly. "Trying to organize other people's lives is a bad habit I have left over from my previous existence. Your mother's just about broken me of it, but every once in a while I slip up." He leaned forward.

"You're having a pretty hard time of it, aren't you, Raine? Being forced to make important decisions with all the gossips nipping at your heels. I know what that's like. I've been through it. It's pretty intense while you're the center of it, but it does die down…eventually. Something else happens and attention moves on."

"I want it to go away *now*."

"I know."

"We had to tell Annabelle about the baby yesterday. She cornered us when we went out for a walk."

"There's an advantage to having it all come out at once."

"It's over with sooner, I know. Gabe thinks that, too."

George reached for his empty pipe, sucked on it a second or two, then said, "I spoke to Gabe yesterday morning."

Raine looked up. "You did? What about?"

George motioned vaguely with his pipe. "Everything that's going on."

Raine lifted her chin. "Do you think I'm taking advantage of him, too?"

George was silent, then he said slowly, "It's been my experience that a man seldom volunteers for something he doesn't want to do." He paused. "How do you feel about Gabe, Raine? I mean now, today?"

Raine searched for words. "Grateful, appreciative…"

"Do you think he's comfortable with that? That that's what he wants?"

Raine's frown deepened. "I don't understand. What do you—"

"I'm doing it again, aren't I? Well, never mind.

People are best served when left alone to find their own way.'' George smiled again and surprised her by reaching over and patting her hand. ''I have to tell you the truth, Raine,'' he said. ''When I married your mother, I had misgivings about how you and I were going to get along. You'd had her all to yourself for most of your life. She doted on you. All the time she worked so hard, it was for you. She wanted the best for you— dancing lessons, voice training…anything you wanted. Maybe I came to be jealous of you when I fell in love with your mother, I don't know. She did talk about you a lot—Raine this, Raine that. I didn't want to share her. And I didn't know you very well…I *still* don't know you very well.'' He laughed softly. ''But the resentment's gone away. You're important to Marge, so you're important to me. What happens to you matters. I want the best for you, Raine. Just the same as if you were one of my own children.''

It was strange how a simple act of kindness from an unexpected source was sometimes harder to deal with than the meanness and criticism of known enemies.

''I—I'll remember that,'' Raine said huskily.

He nodded and sat back, his teeth clamping down on his pipe stem.

RAINE DIDN'T WAIT for her mother's return. She went back to Gabe's house, oddly satisfied by her exchange with George—feeling that they'd taken several giant steps forward in cementing their relationship.

Truth to tell, she'd been a bit jealous of him as well. Having to share her mother was difficult for her, even though she was no longer a child and not living at home. It was the *idea* that was difficult to accept.

Now, having talked with George without the filter of her mother's presence, she could easily see what had attracted her to him in the first place. He was a genuinely nice man, strong and kind and basically nonjudgmental. His first instinct was to heal.

Raine was still confused, though, by what George had meant in what he'd said about Gabe. What did her feelings for Gabe have to do with Gabe's comfort? With what *he* wanted? He simply wanted to help her; that was the way it was with them. He knew her inside and out, just as she knew him.

Only…did she? She'd known him in childhood and through their teen years, but she'd left Tyler when he was twenty-two and just out of the community college in Sugar Creek. Today he was almost thirty. Seven years was a long time in a person's life—he'd said that himself.

She shook her head. No. He was still very much the old Gabe she'd always known. Sweet and kind and loyal.

Seven years! another part of her mind insisted. She had changed during that time, moved from being a girl to a woman. What changes had those years wrought in Gabe? Had she been too embroiled in her own problems even to begin to notice?

She stood in the doorway to his bedroom. She hadn't given particular heed to the room before, but now her gaze took in everything. She'd known it all her life, lived with its various evolutions as Gabe changed from a young boy to a young man. Star Wars and Star Trek posters had been replaced with

posters of his favorite rock bands and scantily clad
models. Several years before she left for New York
the decor had changed yet again, reflecting a growing
sophistication. All the juvenile posters had come
down, the curtains changed from print to a solid
color, the bookshelves swept of all but the most precious keepsakes.

Presently, the room had lost all vestiges of youth.
It was a man's room, decorated with a good eye for
color and comfort. The bed had been switched from
twin to double; the walls were painted a deep shade
of blue, the woodwork a glossy white.

Raine's throat tightened. It was so different from
what she remembered that it was like looking at the
reflection of a stranger!

"Gabe?" she whispered. But the empty room gave
her no answer.

CHAPTER EIGHT

GABE WAS TO HAVE the next day off, according to
the schedule he kept on the kitchen calendar, and
Raine had gone to sleep glad in the knowledge that
they would be together. She'd remained mildly unsettled through the remainder of the day. Gabe was
a relied-upon rock in her world. Even the smallest
possibility of change was disturbing. She needed to
see him again, talk to him, to reassure herself that he
was still the same. But when she dragged herself out
of bed the next morning, after a night filled with
dreams, it was to find a note from him stuck to the
refrigerator door.

> Red,
> I forgot to tell you. I promised to help Alyssa
> Wocheck with a project this morning. Can't get
> out of it. Should be through by two. Think about
> what you'd like to do then. How about a ride
> out to Timber Lake?
> Gabe

Raine dropped the note on the table and went to
stare out the window. She wasn't accustomed to being so alone. In New York there was always something to do and someone to do it with. She had her

friends and had made friends with a number of Joel's.

Here in Tyler, she was beginning to feel useless. Other than doing her stretches and exercises to keep her body strong and supple, she had little to keep herself occupied. The house was in tip-top shape and simple maintenance was all it needed.

She went over to the goldfish bowl and sprinkled in some food. As usual, Frederica gobbled it up, flicking her beautiful tail and fins to dart from flake to flake.

The telephone rang and Raine jumped, an indication of the taut state of her nerves. She lifted the receiver just before the answering machine switched on. "Hello?" she said, hoping that the caller would be someone she would want to speak to.

"Raine?" A familiar voice said her name.

"Roger?" Raine replied, instantly identifying him.

He laughed. It was a nice laugh, quietly masculine, yet filled with genuine humor. "It's been so long since we talked I wasn't sure you'd remember. Did Dad tell you I'd call?"

"He mentioned something about it, yes. But it hasn't been that long. I wouldn't forget."

"Four years."

"No!" she said in disbelief.

"Four years," he confirmed. "I've had my practice here for two."

"I still can't believe... How are you?" she asked warmly.

"Better than the last time we met. That's what I'm calling about. When do you think we could have lunch together again?"

"I'm free today."

There was a silence, during which Raine wished she hadn't jumped at the opportunity so quickly.

"Well, as luck would have it," Roger said momentarily, "so am I, so that's perfect. How about Timberlake Lodge at noon?"

"Sounds good to me. I'll be there."

"Uh...you know Gabe's welcome, too."

Raine wound the curly telephone cord around her finger. "He won't be here," she said.

"He's at work?" Roger asked.

"No, he's off doing something. For Alyssa, I believe."

"Ah, Alyssa...yes."

A dog started barking in the background and suddenly a number of others joined in.

Raine laughed. "Are you in a kennel?" she asked.

"The clinic," he answered. "What you hear are my clients."

"Sounds as if you're doing fairly well."

"I'll tell you all about it later. Noon. Timberlake," he reiterated.

"I'll be there," Raine promised, and as she hung up she found herself smiling. That was the way she always reacted after contact with Roger. His enthusiasm and enjoyment of life was infectious. Even during the dark patch of his parents' divorce and the rumor-filled months that followed, he'd always found something to joke about.

She looked at her watch. It was almost eleven-thirty. She would have to hurry to get ready.

JUST AS GABE HAD DONE, she left a note. In all likelihood, she would be back by two, but she didn't want him to come home early and wonder. She was also going to take the Explorer, which a quick check had shown to be in the garage, and she didn't want him to wonder about that, either.

It felt good to dress up. To put on a nice skirt and blouse, stockings and heels, to wear makeup. It felt good to be going someplace to meet a friend.

Timberlake Lodge had undergone an amazing change since she had known it as a child. It had gone from a private holding of the Ingalls family, in sore need of repair, to part of the Addison Hotel chain, with all the attendant remodeling and sprucing up. Employees in uniform scurried about making guests feel welcome, both in the hotel and at the restaurant. Raine had been amazed the last time she had come for dinner with her mother and George and was still amazed today.

Roger met her in the lobby, getting up from the long low couch where he'd been waiting and taking her hands. He looked her up and down and gave a soft whistle. "Hot stuff!" he teased.

Raine grinned and returned the compliment. "Not bad yourself, Doctor."

After Gabe, she'd always thought Roger Phelps the best catch of their age group. Extremely nice looking, with even features, a square jaw, light brown hair and brown eyes, he managed to be both boyishly mischievous and devilishly attractive in the same breath.

"Do you mind if we skip going to the bar and get a table instead?" he asked. "I have to be back in Sugar Creek at one-thirty to fill in for another vet."

"Not at all," Raine said.

As they followed the hostess to a table halfway across the large room, Raine was aware that several local people were in attendance and that their eyes were tracing their every step.

Roger saw her into her chair, and as he took his own, he flashed a smile. "Just like old times," he said, tongue very firmly in cheek.

Raine looked around at the opulence of their surroundings, at the white tablecloths and stylish, fresh-flower centerpieces. "All we're missing are the roaches," she retorted. Neither of them had had very much money four or five years ago—he in school, she with only an occasional short-term job on stage to supplement her meager income from waitressing. The places they'd eaten were nowhere near as nice as this.

He laughed. "I could say those were the good old days, but I won't. They weren't particularly good for either of us."

"I was happier than you. I was where I wanted to be."

"Yeah, I guess you were."

"I talked with your dad last night. He doesn't seem to mind that you're a vet. In fact, he's proud of you. He told me about your part in reporting the F and M fire."

He shrugged, dismissing his action. "It wasn't all that much."

"Still, he's proud of you."

"The 'new' George Phelps," Roger said. "It took him a while to come around, but it's to his credit that he did. That and your mom. I think she pointed out to him how he was being just a tad hypocritical, considering the huge changes he'd made in his life."

"He said she's a good influence on him."

Their waiter came and they placed their orders.

Afterward, each sat back and studied the other. There was a new maturity about Roger that Raine had never seen before. An underlying seriousness. Before, she'd always sensed a battle taking place deep within him—a battle that revolved around his relationship with his father. That situation seemed to have resolved itself, both because of his father's mellowing and because Roger was at last following the course he himself had chosen.

"You like caring for animals, don't you?" she said. "I never knew that was what you wanted. You never said."

He shrugged again. "I didn't think there was much use talking about it. Dad was determined I go to med school and nothing else seemed to matter."

"Had you ever told him?" she asked, curious.

"I tried. He didn't listen very well back then, and I—" his brown eyes twinkled "—I was ready to use any excuse to get out of Tyler, just like you."

"Why did you come back then?" she questioned.

"It just sort of happened. Old Dr. Stewart was retiring and I took over his practice."

She nodded. She wanted to ask about Roger's marital status, whether he was still single, engaged or married to someone she might or might not know, but her own precarious position in that area stopped her. She played with the stem of her water glass and tried to come up with another topic.

"You're looking well," he said, his brown eyes steady.

Raine nodded stiffly. Here it comes! she thought. As an active businessman in Tyler, Roger had to have heard the gossip.

"Would you rather not talk about it?" he asked quietly.

A pensive smile flickered across her mouth. "I can't seem to do anything else. It's all everyone wants to discuss."

"Then we won't," he decided.

She shook her head. "No. It doesn't matter. Not really. And of everyone in town, I'd rather talk to you."

The soup they'd ordered was served, but Roger ignored it. He leaned forward to take her hand and repeated what he'd heard. "You and Gabe are married. And there's a baby on the way."

Raine nodded. Technically, Roger was a member of her immediate family, but she couldn't bring herself to tell him the entire truth. She didn't want to burden him with it.

"So what's the problem?" he asked.

She glanced around at the people who still watched them. She sensed their interest in Roger's attention to her, as well as their building disapproval. She withdrew her hand from his and slipped it under the table. "No one expected it. Don't tell me you don't find it a little surprising as well."

"It was sudden, but things happen that way sometime," he said.

"It was more than sudden," she contradicted.

He frowned, his gaze moving to the people covertly and not so covertly watching them.

"Folks here like a good gossip."

"And Gabe and I are giving it to them."

"I have to admit," he said honestly, "I was a little surprised. But you and he always were close."

Raine laughed hollowly.

Roger's frown deepened. "Raine—"

Someone bumped against the table, hitting it hard enough to almost spill the soup.

"Hey! Watch it!" Roger reacted sharply.

A nice-looking man in his late thirties, dressed in tan pants, a flannel shirt and a multipocketed tan vest covered with emblems, immediately apologized. "Oh, I'm sorry. I didn't mean to… I was looking for some friends and wasn't watching where I—" He broke off when he got a better look at Raine's table companion. "Roger?"

Roger smiled and got to his feet. "I hardly recognized you," he said, extending his hand.

The intruder accepted it enthusiastically. "That's because I'm here on *important* business."

Roger raised a skeptical eyebrow, then introduced Raine. "Paul, this is Raine Peterson…er, Atwood. Raine…Paul Chambers, the newest member of our medical community. His specialty is pediatrics. In fact, you might—"

"I've heard a lot about you," she said, offering her hand as well.

Paul Chambers smiled. "Only good things, I hope."

"Of course." She slipped her hand back under the table.

"What's going on?" Roger asked, sitting down again. "What kind of *important* business? Fishing?"

Paul grinned. "The best pastime known to mankind—fly-fishing." The lodge is hosting a conference later this month and I'm here, at tremendous sacrifice to myself, mind you, to meet with some of the conference committee members and help them preview the area. Sheila Lawson set it up."

Roger smiled. "Yes, it looks like a tremendous sacrifice."

"Taking the afternoon off, being forced to commune with nature, possibly catching a few fish..." He sighed. "Will this torture never end?"

Roger made a show of replacing his napkin. "I truly feel sorry for you," he said dryly.

"Believe me," Paul said, growing serious, "I know how lucky I am." He turned to Raine with a smile. "Nice to meet you." Then, spotting the people he was supposed to meet, he excused himself and made his way over to a table in the corner, where two men and a woman, all dressed similarly to him, waited.

"I was going to say, you might like to consider him as your baby's pediatrician. He comes highly recommended," Roger said.

"Your father has already recommended him."

"Oh."

Raine toyed with her soup. "What about you?" she asked eventually, returning to her earlier unasked question. "Are you married yet, or engaged?"

"Still as free as the birds in the trees."

"Not for want of looking, though," she guessed.

"No, I look. I just haven't found what I want yet."

"What do you want?" she asked.

"I don't know," he said with a laugh. "But I'm sure I'll know when I find it...or rather, her. Right now my best girl is a golden retriever named Serra. She was abused and abandoned, and I'm doing my best to find her a good home. Say, would you be interested in—"

"No, we have a fish, thank you. That's enough at the moment."

The main course was served and they started to eat, purposely keeping their conversation light. Both refused dessert, and soon they were strolling through the hotel's main doors to the parking area.

Roger's Saturn was parked close to Gabe's Explorer.

"This was nice," he said. "Let's don't let it be so long before we do it again."

"Yes," Raine agreed. Then on impulse, she gave him a hug. Only to find when she drew away that one or two of the people who had been most interested in herself and Roger in the restaurant were passing by.

Roger followed her gaze. "Maybe we'd better be sure to invite Gabe next time," he murmured, teasing.

Raine tried to smile but found it difficult. Why did everything have to be so complicated? Couldn't life be simple once in a while? A friend lunching with a friend!

She started to turn away, ready to fit the key into the door lock, when Roger stopped her. "Raine?" he said, once again serious. "Let me know if there's anything I can do, okay?"

Raine nodded, unable to speak.

"And tell Gabe," he continued, "tell Gabe he's a very lucky man."

GABE SAT at the kitchen table, waiting. While he was helping Alyssa at least four people had rushed up to him with the news that Raine was having lunch with Roger Phelps at Timberlake Lodge. It was also there in her note. "I'm meeting Roger for lunch. Taking the car to the lodge. Raine.'' He knew he shouldn't be jealous, but he was.

They were acting very friendly, he'd been told. *Holding hands…a kiss afterward.*

Some years ago Roger had lived in New York, at the same time as Raine. They'd had frequent contact, Marge had told him, glad that her daughter had had someone from home to talk to occasionally. Two years ago Roger had come back to Tyler to practice veterinary medicine. But did that mean all contact between the two of them had ceased?

Could Roger be the baby's father?

A car pulled into the driveway and stopped—the Explorer. Raine hopped out, walked to the kitchen door and let herself in.

Gabe didn't move. He stayed at the table, trying to control his emotions.

She broke into a bright smile when she saw him. ''Gabe! You're home! I thought maybe I…'' She glanced at her watch to check the time.

''I came home early,'' he said levelly. She had looked so happy coming into the house. Then upon seeing him—it might have been his imagination, he couldn't be sure—she'd seemed to tighten up inside in spite of her smile.

''I was having lunch with Roger. Did you see my…'' She glanced at the note lying crumpled on the table. She looked back at him.

Gabe knew he couldn't continue to behave this way. He had no hold on her, either in the past or the present. They might be married, but the vows had no force. She didn't know that he loved her, that the thought of her being with another man—especially now—cut into him like a knife.

"I heard. Several people made it their business to tell me. They thought it might be something more than a lunch." He forced himself to loosen up, even smile. "I reminded them that you were stepbrother and sister...and if it didn't bother me, why should it bother them?"

Her smile returned. "I knew we were being watched. It's so disgusting when people put two and two together and come up with five. It was a simple lunch, that's all. He's a friend."

"From your New York days." The words leaped out of their own volition.

"I haven't seen him for four years!"

"So he's not the baby's father?"

"Hardly!" She laughed, then noticed that he hadn't. Her body stiffened—ever so slightly, but he was aware of it. She shook her head. "No, he's not the baby's father. Is that why you..." She motioned to the note.

A muscle jumped along his jawline. "I can't be blamed for wondering," he said.

Raine pulled a chair from its usual place at the side of the table and scooted it close to his. When she sat in it, their knees almost touched.

She had gone all out for this lunch with Roger, Gabe noted—hose, high heels, carefully applied makeup. She didn't look like the "Tyler" Raine. She looked like "New York"—stylish, sophisticated, someone completely out of his sphere. But she was watching him carefully, as if what he thought made a huge difference to her, as if she dreaded his possible rejection.

"I'll tell you if you really want to know," she said

quietly. "He's someone I met while rehearsing for a musical. I was in the chorus, and he—"

Gabe stopped her. It was too much. At this particular moment, it was far too much! "No, I don't want to know."

"I'd have told you if it was Roger, Gabe," she said sincerely. "I wouldn't have expected you to meet him in town and not be aware that he was the father. Anyway, you two are friends, aren't you?"

"To some degree. We played sports together in high school. But after that, he wasn't here much."

"It still would have been wrong for me not to tell you."

Her green eyes held his, hopeful and pleading. When she looked at him like that, Gabe acknowledged, he could deny her nothing. He brought her head to rest lightly against his chest and held it there, his own eyes, hidden from her view, closing. If anything, he loved her more.

She stirred, but instead of pushing away, she wrapped her arms around his waist, securing their closeness.

"You're still the same, aren't you, Gabe?" she whispered tightly. "I need you to be the same. Not to have changed. You are comfortable with what we've done, aren't you? And if—if it ever comes to be that you aren't...you'll tell me right away, won't you? You won't wait?"

"I promise," Gabe said, and when she straightened she gave him a wavery smile.

When he was once again alone in the kitchen, Raine having gone to change into something more appropriate for hiking over the rolling hills beside Timber Lake, Gabe thought about the future. No firm date had been set for anything after the birth. How long would they stay together? And after they parted, would she and the baby eventually go back to New York? Other dancers had children, yet still found a way to work on the stage.

The baby. The growing child. What would his relationship with it be? Would he see it more than just the occasional time when Raine came back to Tyler to visit? Would the child know him only as Gabe, the nice man who lived next door?

And what of Raine? When this sham of a marriage was over, would she drift back under the influence of the man who had impregnated her, then rejected her? Or would she move on to someone else?

What if instead… No! He shook his head, denying the thought. But it was so compelling, so tantalizing, that he couldn't refute it altogether. Would it be possible…*could* it be possible…that Raine—after a time, after a long time—might come to love him? And if not fully love him, at least be willing to stay married to him, so that the child might have a caring, attentive father? In name, if not in blood?

The idea stayed with Gabe all through the afternoon as they tramped about the hills surrounding Timber Lake. If only there was a way he could make Raine see him as something other than her good buddy Gabe. She needed him now. She wanted him close. But that was as far as it went. He ached to hold her, to tell her of his love. But he held the emotion back. The quickest way to send her running was to reveal too much of himself. What she needed from him, trusted him to give her, was stability in an unsteady world. For the moment all he could do was continue to bide his time.

CHAPTER NINE

MARGE PAID A CALL shortly after they returned from the lake to ask them over for dinner that night.

"I don't quite know how this happened," she said briskly. "It's not something I planned, but one thing led to another, and now dinner for four has turned into a crowd! And all of them want to see you! Britt and Jake, Nora and Byron, Susannah and Joe... I'm going to have to make a run to the diner for more food! I know it's late notice," Marge continued, sensing her daughter's hesitation, "but if you can possibly do it, you should come. They're your and Gabe's friends, Raine. They're not going to make impolite comments."

Gabe waited for Raine to make the decision. "Sure. Why not?" she said, reluctantly agreeing.

Marge hurried to the door. "At seven. Okay?"

"Is there anything we can bring?" Raine asked.

"Not a thing," Marge called over her shoulder as she stepped outside. "Just yourselves."

Gabe checked the clock on the wall. "Not much time," he said.

"The story of my day," Raine murmured.

"You want to take first shower?"

"Maybe I'd better. It took six tries before I found something that fit comfortably for lunch!"

"You could wear that again," he said. "It looked nice."

Raine paused in the doorway. Men—they just didn't have a clue. "I'll find something else," she assured him, smiling. "Don't worry. I was exaggerating. I haven't grown out of all my clothes...yet."

"It won't make any difference when you do. You're going to be beautiful all the way through this."

Raine thought of Joel, of the disparaging way he talked about dancers who took time out to have children. "Little better than cows!" he'd fumed. "Don't they see what they're doing to themselves?" His idea of beauty was diametrically opposed to Gabe's....

Gabe frowned. "What's the matter? You looked funny all of a sudden."

She shook her head. Joel was out of her life, at least at the present. She didn't have to think about him, consider his views. In the future...? "I was just thinking about what you said," she answered honestly. "We'll check back to see if you still feel that way in four or five months, when I start to resemble the Goodyear blimp!"

"I'll still feel the same," he said steadily.

She rolled her eyes before starting off down the hall.

"I will!" he called after her, then teased, "Remember those old models we used to make when we were kids? I've always had a fascination for blimps."

"You're hopeless, Gabe!" she retorted before shutting herself in the bathroom.

His answering chuckle carried down the hall.

RAINE HAD BEEN exaggerating, but she wasn't too far off the mark when she'd said she was going to have a hard time finding something to wear. Last week her skirts and slacks had fit a little snugly. This week, the seams strained on all but a couple of choices: the skirt she'd worn for lunch, and a soft summery dress with a fashionably high waist and long floaty skirt that was designed for freedom of movement. She pulled the skirt of the summery dress taut over what had once been her flat tummy and saw the tiny bulge. There was nothing for it. It was only going to get bigger.

She turned sideways, still holding the dress taut, and looked at herself in the mirror. Raine Peterson, baby maker. It still didn't feel real, just as being Gabe's wife didn't feel real. It was like the game she'd insisted on playing when they were children: mommy, daddy and baby. Only the doll they'd used had been replaced by a real baby she was busily creating. In a little more than six short months it would be here, and then... She let the dress fall back into place. And then she would be faced with the need to make even more decisions.

She heard the shower switch off and Gabe pad barefoot to his room. To save time, while he was getting dressed, she would brush her teeth and apply her makeup and surprise him by being ready when he was.

She opened the bedroom door, ready to step into the hall. At that exact same instant the door across the hall opened and Gabe, wearing only a towel draped loosely about his hips, stood facing her.

Raine's gasp was instinctive. It had been years since she had seen him with so little on. Not since summers at the lake, when they and some of their friends had spent hours lolling about in the water and on the float just offshore from the old Timberlake Lodge. Swimsuits had been the dress of the day—Speedos for the boys and bikinis for the girls. The idea had been to wear as little as possible in order to show off their supple young bodies.

But this! This was wholly different. Where before Gabe had been a slender, athletic boy on the brink of maturity, he now was a fully grown male—still slender, still athletic, but harder, with sculpted muscles in his shoulders and chest and abdomen. His lean look when dressed was deceptive, Raine realized, running her eyes down his frame, to slim hips and long, powerful thighs. His shirt and slacks hid the body of an excellently conditioned man. A fire fighter who could, if need be, throw a person over his shoulder, make his way through a smoke-filled building, climb out a window and down an extension ladder—all without blinking an eye!

He seemed just as startled as she. Frozen, almost. Neither of them spoke. Then, sounding slightly rattled, he said, "You need back in the bathroom?"

"N-no, I—I was just..." Ridiculously, she felt herself blush. She was a pregnant woman, for heaven's sake. She hadn't gotten that way through osmosis! She knew what a nude man looked like. Yet, with Gabe... "...brush my teeth," she mumbled disconnectedly.

Gabe smiled tightly. "I forgot something. I'll be out in a minute. Want me to tap on the door?"

Raine couldn't collect her thoughts well enough to do anything but refuse. When in doubt, say no—that was what her mother used to tell her. Possibly if she'd paid proper heed to that advice in the previous months she wouldn't be in such a predicament now. "No," she said, "I'll hear you. No rush."

Gabe smiled that special Gabe smile and Raine felt her heart give a little flutter. She immediately closed the door. With her pulse still pounding, she waited a full five minutes after hearing him close his door before she again ventured into the hall.

RAINE WAS SURE the dinner was up to her mother's usual standard, yet she couldn't have sworn to it in a court of law. She went through the motions of eating, but didn't register the taste of anything. She smiled and made all the appropriate responses to the conversation taking place around her, but it might have been someone else sitting in her chair, borrowing her body.

Why had she reacted as she had to seeing Gabe in such an intimate light? Yes, he was a man. Yes, she was a woman. But that didn't automatically elicit a physical attraction. She was accustomed to seeing beautiful bodies on both men and women. Dancers honed their physiques as they perfected their abilities. Muscles had to be trained and conditioned and then kept in shape. Body-hugging clothing allowed free movement, kept working muscles warm. Very little was left to the imagination.

So why had she reacted so strongly to Gabe? Was it the unexpectedness of coming upon him wearing so little? The fact that he was Gabe...and yet not Gabe, because he no longer had the body of the boy she remembered. Because, to her shocked surprise, that boy had changed into a very sexy man?

Gabe?

She remembered the way she had scurried back

into her room, the way her heart had pounded. From
shock? From surprise? She hadn't been prepared. It
was like suddenly realizing that a person you thought
you knew wasn't really that person, after all!

She chanced a quick glance down the length of the
crowded table. Gabe was near the end, talking with
Joe Santori. Compared to Joe's workman brawn,
Gabe's slimness was pronounced. So, too, were his
gentler features. Joe was vibrant, with curly black
hair, black eyes and a strong Italianate face. His
voice boomed in a mellow baritone; his laugh was
strong, infectious. Gabe was naturally quieter, in
looks and personality.

Joe's wife was seated on Raine's immediate left.
Leaning close, Susannah murmured, "Joe is so proud
of the remodeling work he did on this house. It was
a joy for him to work with your mother and George.
If you and Gabe and Gabe's dad should ever want
to add on to your place—"

"Joe will be our first choice for contractor, of
course," Raine replied.

Susannah grinned. She was a small, dainty woman
with a delicate face and huge, thickly lashed blue
eyes. "I'm not trying to drum up business, even
though it sounds like it, doesn't it? It's just... Joe
likes to see families stay together. And there's been
so many break apart recently."

"Because of the F and M?" Raine asked.

Susannah nodded. "Things were starting to get
better. People were actually beginning to gain a little
ground. Then the fire happened." She sighed. "Has
Gabe heard anything that the rest of us haven't? Has
the insurance company made a ruling yet?"

Raine shook her head. "No."

Britt leaned over from Raine's right. "This dessert of your mother's is fabulous," she said. "She's not planning to go into competition with Yes! Yogurt, is she?"

Marge overheard. "Absolutely not! This is just something I found a recipe for and wanted to try."

When they moved from the table to the living room, Nora Gates Forrester sat on the couch next to Raine. "What do you think of your mother's new look?" she asked.

"I like it," Raine said, watching her mother laugh at something Jake Marshack said.

"She's a new woman since she married George," Nora continued. "It was a good thing. Even the worst of the gossips agree about that now."

"Gossips!" Raine said disparagingly under her breath.

Nora, a woman who had always been fiercely independent, nodded, her ash-blond hair swinging. "I love Cece, but her mother has to be *the* worst..." She paused and looked at Raine closely. "Try not to let it bother you, all right?"

That was the nearest anyone had come that evening to mentioning the gossip swirling around town. Everyone had acted happy to see Gabe and her and were accepting of their marriage. If they had questions about the suddenness of the act, they kept them to themselves.

A short time later Gabe came over and, taking Raine's hand, pulled her from the couch. "It's time we left," he said quietly.

Raine couldn't stifle a yawn. For the past fifteen minutes she'd been fighting a mostly losing battle to keep her eyes open.

"Oh, wait!" Britt cried, jumping up. "The present. Don't leave until..." She motioned Byron forward.

Byron, a transplant from New England, whose innate quality of educated sophistication had yet to be pierced by life in a small Midwestern town, reached into his pocket and withdrew an envelope, which he handed to Gabe.

Gabe undid the flap and pulled out a greeting card. Tucked inside were mock-ups of two airline tickets and several shiny tourist brochures of hotels in the Bahamas. The card seemed to have been signed by a majority of the people in Tyler. Names and personal remembrances covered it, front and back.

"It's a honeymoon!" Britt said excitedly. "All you have to do is let Peggy, over at Tyler Travel, know when you want to go, and she'll take it from there."

"We tried to think what you might like," Nora said, "and this was the result."

"It's good for a year," Susannah added.

There was a tiny silence as all waited for a reaction from Gabe and Raine. Raine swallowed and blinked.

"This...we're overwhelmed!" she claimed.

"All these people?" Gabe asked tightly, skimming the multitude of names.

Britt grinned. "That's what you get for being such a great guardian angel, Gabe."

"An archangel," Marge corrected. "Gabriel, the herald of good news."

The men thumped Gabe on the back. "Think you'll be able to tear yourself away from Tyler for a week?" Joe Santori joked.

"But this is too much!" Gabe protested.

A short time later, after more good wishes, they escaped from the house.

"The Bahamas!" Raine murmured as they crossed the yard.

"For a week," Gabe said.

"We'll hurt their feelings if we don't go, and yet..."

Gabe opened the kitchen door and held it for her. He said nothing. Once inside the house he still said nothing, and as the silence lengthened, Raine's nerves grew more taut.

This had not been a particularly great day for her, either. She paced from one side of the room to the other.

"So what do you want to do," she challenged him, irritated with his seeming withdrawal, "give it back? What will we tell them? 'Sorry, we can't accept this because our marriage is a sham'? And sham marriages shouldn't be celebrated with expensive wedding presents?"

Gabe looked at her, his clear eyes steady. Then he said huskily, "Come here, Red," and held out his arms.

Raine slipped into place against him, like a lost puppy finding refuge in a storm. Her emotions were in turmoil. She wanted to cry, she wanted to laugh, but was afraid either could turn into hysteria.

"I told you the people here were basically good," he said softly, above her ear.

"It was easier when I thought they were awful!" she moaned. "Why did they have to do that, Gabe? Why did they have to do something nice? And I'm not meaning the people we're close to. I mean the others. The ones who... I feel terrible now."

Gabe shrugged, having no answer.

His arms felt so comforting wrapped around her, his body so... Raine pushed away abruptly. She kept her gaze down.

"Red?" he murmured, obviously surprised.

"I'm tired, Gabe. I want to go to bed...to sleep. It's been... Today..."

He backed away, arms extended widely in a gesture of capitulation. "Whatever you want," he said.

She turned, only to stop and glance back. "I'm sorry, Gabe. I just...I'm really very tired. I—I enjoyed our walk at the lake today."

He nodded, but she could sense his confusion. He knew something had happened, but he didn't know what.

Raine closed herself in the bedroom, only to resume her pacing. She knew the "what," but not the "why." It involved her earlier recognition of Gabe as a man who had feelings, emotions and needs. A sensual man...sexual, attractive to women. Like discovering that your youngest brother was sleeping with his teenage girlfriend, it came as a shock to the system. Only in this case, Gabe wasn't her real brother. And just now, when he'd held her...

Raine hurried to the closet, where she tore off her dress and exchanged it for a nightgown. She'd have liked to brush her teeth again, but she wasn't about to take the chance of meeting Gabe in the hall.

SUNDAY WAS Gabe's last shift before he had four days off. He hadn't disturbed her sleep when he left for work shortly before seven that morning, but she found a note in the kitchen. "Hope you feel better today. Gabe." Beside the note was a plate of fresh sweet rolls that he must have gone out early to buy. The coffeemaker was also set up and ready to go. All she had to do was switch it on.

Dear, sweet Gabe, she thought.

Today she wasn't going to think about last night. This was another day. A time for new thoughts, new experiences, when shimmers of emotion could be ignored. When looking ahead was far and away the best...

Yeah, right! her more cynical self asserted.

Raine sighed and a short time later, poured herself a cup of coffee. It still didn't make sense to her. How could she possibly feel what she had for Gabe? Was the tingle of physical attraction another side effect of her pregnancy? Was it because he was the father figure to her baby and she was unconsciously trying to bond to him? Was it loneliness? Was she missing Joel? Once, she'd thought she loved him. Now her feelings were taking on a distinct aura of anger. She'd given six months of her life to him! Subjugated her wants for his. She must have been temporarily insane! Even though he was Joel Hastings—big man in the New York theater, highly talented, deeply charming—he hadn't stood behind her when she'd needed him. Hadn't supported her.

The telephone rang, interrupting her thoughts. The answering machine switched on and she heard Gabe's voice give its usual message. After the beep, a woman spoke.

"Ah, hello...Raine? Raine, this is Maureen Wilson. I work with Gabe. I don't know if you remember me, but we went to school together. We were in a couple of talent shows. I sang and did the hula." She laughed uncomfortably. "Not very well, but I did it.

What I'm calling about is…do you think you could come by the station around three this afternoon? If you can, and if you can let me know soon enough, I'll call the others who are off duty and they'll come in, too. We want to give Gabe and you a little party. Gabe doesn't know anything about it. We'd like to surprise him.'' She paused, as if running through a mental checklist. "Well, I think that's it. Call me at the station.'' She hung up, and a few seconds later the machine switched off.

Raine stared at the blinking light that indicated a recorded message. Now there were even more people who wanted to be nice to them. She was tempted not to return the call, but that would only cause a postponement in their plans, not a cancellation. She dialed the number of the station Gabe had posted prominently on a notepad, apologized to Maureen for missing her call and agreed to be present at three. Maureen's glad response was in direct contrast to Raine's disquiet, but Maureen never knew it.

RAINE WAS DETERMINED to be bright and effervescent at the fire station that afternoon. These were Gabe's friends, his co-workers. The last thing she wanted to do was embarrass him in front of them by behaving as if something had upset her.

She was just being silly, she told herself as she clawed her way back to a more positive frame of mind. She shouldn't look at the situation too closely. Just let it be. Nothing had changed in the balance of her and Gabe's friendship.

She washed the dress she had worn to dinner last night, altered the look slightly with a pair of white sandals and a white hair band and set off for the fire station.

It was a beautiful spring Sunday afternoon, one of the best Tyler had to offer. The sun was shining, birds were singing, a few people were mowing their lawns. Without her being fully aware of it, Raine's forced pose of relaxation became reality. Several people driving by tooted their horns and waved at her; others working in their front yards called their hellos. No one looked at her rudely or pointedly. Either the wonderful weather had affected them, too, or their ministers had delivered a morning sermon about the ills of passing judgment too quickly and they had taken it to heart.

Maureen met Raine at the rear of the fire station and sneaked her inside while someone distracted Gabe.

"All we can hope is that we don't get called out in the next half hour or so," Maureen said, grinning.

Raine had remembered Maureen as soon as she saw her. She hadn't changed all that much since high school. One grade her junior, Maureen had always given Raine the impression of extreme competence along with a keen sense of fun. The mock hula she'd referred to in her message had been the hit of the talent show because it had been done with rollicking good humor.

"Raine...hello!" Chief Sorenson came out of his office to greet her. "It's been years since you and Becky used to run around together. Has Gabe told you what Becky's up to now? Wants to be a helicopter pilot. I had a fit when she told me, but her mom egged her on. Now I can see why. The girl seems to have a knack for it. All her evaluations have been excellent! She's at the top of her class.''

"We'd better get you hidden,'' Maureen murmured, interrupting them. "Richard can't keep Gabe outside forever.''

The chief grimaced. "We'll talk later,'' he promised.

Other fire fighters had started to assemble in the large room, which had many of the comforts of home—couches, chairs, a television, a long trestle table, a kitchen off to one side.

Maureen and Raine slipped into Chief Sorenson's office and Maureen shut the blinds. "It'll only be a couple of minutes,'' she said, cocking her head to listen.

Raine heard even more people gather in the outer room, then the assembly grew quiet. Soon Raine heard Gabe's voice. He was talking with another man…then someone shouted, a cheer went up and any number of people seemed to be talking at once. Without waiting another second, Maureen hurried Raine out the door and into the pandemonium.

Gabe was still recovering from his surprise when he saw her and was surprised all over again. Maureen rushed her over to his side as smiling faces surrounded them.

"Congratulations!'' someone shouted.

"To Gabe and Raine!'' someone else called, holding high a small plastic bottle of mountain spring water.

Gabe tucked an arm around Raine and pulled her close to his side as more bottles of water were passed through the crowd and raised.

"Many happy years together!'' came the toast.

"Kiss the bride!" someone urged, a request that was taken up by a number of others.

Gabe looked at Raine, lifted an eyebrow, then kissed her full on the lips. Not a short kiss, either. One long enough to please the crowd.

Raine heard the laughter, heard the good-natured catcalls, heard the whistles...then he was drawing away and she was left to smile widely, shake out-thrust hands and receive other kisses on the cheek. She tried to tell herself that this entire affair was an act. She was acting right then, trying to pretend that she was a normal bride, that Gabe was a normal groom, that the kiss had been something usual be-tween them. But it wasn't. And she wasn't sure how convincing her performance was at that moment.

Chief Sorenson presented the gift—a silver fruit bowl engraved with their names and the date of their wedding.

"Some of us wanted to give you one of those por-table propane barbecue pits," a man beside them murmured to Gabe, "but we were outvoted."

A sheet cake with the prerequisite toy bride and groom was brought to the table, and Raine's hand and Gabe's were positioned together on the knife. Somehow they managed to cut the first piece, then—mercifully—Maureen took over.

Raine was smiling so hard her cheeks hurt. There were a number of people here she knew and a num-ber of others she didn't. One of the latter—a tall, well-built man with dark hair, dark eyes and rug-gedly handsome features—caught her attention, mostly because he was watching her and Gabe so closely. He held an untouched bottle of water in his hand, and she had yet to see him smile.

As people settled to eat their cake and chat in small groups, Gabe took Raine with him to meet the man, who'd kept apart. He was introduced as Richard Jensen.

"Nice to meet you," the man said as he and Raine touched hands.

"Want some cake?" Gabe asked when he noticed his friend wasn't holding a plate.

"Naah. I'll let the others fight over it."

"How long have they been planning this?" Gabe asked, indicating the party.

"A couple of days. Maureen and Lynn did most of the work."

Gabe shook his head. "I suppose you knew about the other present, too."

"What other present?"

"The trip to the Bahamas."

Slowly, almost begrudgingly, Richard smiled. "Oh, that."

"You knew!"

"Couldn't help knowing. The big debate in the station was whether to go in with that or get something on our own. You're holding what we decided on." He turned his dark gaze to Raine. "You like it?" he asked.

Raine had the oddest feeling that he was asking her much more than that. It wouldn't have surprised her at all if he added, *You going to keep it?* His alert gaze seemed to see a lot. Possibly more than she wanted anyone to know.

She lifted her chin. "I think it's beautiful," she said.

Suddenly the alarm bell rang, accompanied by a chorus of groans.

"Wouldn't you know it!" someone grumbled.

But no one on duty slacked in their responsibility. Like a well-oiled machine, a small cluster of them responded to the call.

Gabe had groaned along with everyone else. Then he yelled to one and all, "Thanks guys! This was great!" before he muttered regretfully to Raine, "Gotta go."

Raine nodded her understanding.

"I wish I could have shown you around the station," he said.

"I'll do it," Richard Jensen volunteered, surprising both Raine and Gabe.

As Raine circulated among those who remained, adding her own thanks to Gabe's—in particular to Maureen and Lynn—she heard the powerful motor of the fire engine come to life, then the wail of its siren as it raced away.

For a moment she wondered what it was like to ride the wind to the source of a fire, to match wits there with one of the most elemental forces in nature. Gabe was trained to do that. Yet he rarely talked about it.

Richard moved silently into place at her side. "The chief said it's okay if I show you around."

Raine nodded. The party was breaking up; it wouldn't be impolite for her to leave. "Where to first?" she asked.

"Since we're up here, here. You know where the chief's office is…" he said, starting off.

For the next fifteen minutes Raine was shown the training room, the dayroom where the party had been held, then downstairs—the dorm where the fire fighters on duty slept at night, the secretary's office and the high-ceilinged expanse where the fire engine and much of the equipment was housed.

Raine looked around, puzzled. "Where's the pole you slide down?" she asked. "Did I miss it?"

Richard unbent enough to smile again. "We've never had a pole. We use the stairs."

Raine blinked. "But don't all firehouses have poles? I mean, isn't it required?"

"Only on TV or in movies."

Raine smiled. "Oh."

"You'll have to come back sometime and let Gabe show you the engine."

"Do you think it was a real fire they went to?" she asked. "Gabe says a lot of the calls you receive are false alarms."

"They won't know till they get there."

She frowned. "It's dangerous work, isn't it?"

"Yes."

"So that part isn't exaggerated in the media."

"No, they get that right."

Raine didn't know whether he was being taciturn because that was the way he was or because he didn't like her. She'd felt a distinct chill all during the tour. With no one about, she decided to meet his resistance head-on. "You don't like me very much, do you, Richard?"

His gaze never wavered. "I don't know you."

"But you know Gabe. You and he are friends."

"Buddies," Richard agreed.

"Gabe's my friend, too," she claimed.

"Glad to hear it."

"You don't believe me?"

Richard's dark eyes narrowed. He was a few years older than Gabe and far more cynical, as if he'd seen more of the world and its harsher elements. "I don't want to see him get hurt."

"Neither do I."

"You could do it, though."

"No—"

He gave a short, disbelieving laugh. "Lady, you could hurt him just by breathing wrong."

"No," Raine declared more vehemently. "I wouldn't—"

A group of fire fighters came straggling down the stairs to the engine area. They were laughing and talking, on their way outside.

Maureen was among them. She veered over to Raine and handed her the silver bowl. "I thought I'd save you the trip back upstairs."

As Raine took the gift she was sure that Richard Jensen attributed a far more negative motive to her neglect than a simple desire to be unencumbered during the tour. "Thanks," she said tightly. It was all she could say. If she tried to defend herself, she would only come off looking worse.

RAINE REFUSED Maureen's offer of a ride home. She would enjoy the walk, she insisted. But she didn't. Because along the way she realized that it wasn't she whom people were being nice to; it was Gabe. And possibly her mother. They were the ones whose roots still ran deep in the Tyler community. Raine was merely an extension of them. For her, personally, there was still suspicion.

On the spur of the moment she stopped off at the grocery store at the town square. Up to now Gabe had been doing most of the cooking on his days off.

Tomorrow she would cook. She would make him a special treat.

She collected a cart and started to push it up and down the aisles, choosing ingredients. She'd remembered that when they were children, Gabe had loved her mother's stuffed chicken. Some months back, after a telephone call home for pointers, Raine had prepared the meal for Joel. He'd eaten it politely but had not been impressed. Gabe would be; Raine was sure.

She had just left the store when Ann Tully passed her on the sidewalk. Gabe had gone back over to the woman's house later the day they'd met, to talk to her unruly son. When he'd come home hours later, he hadn't been very communicative about the boy's current trouble, only expressing hope that all would be well in the end.

"Hello," Raine said, attempting to be friendly.

Ann Tully started. She'd obviously been deep in thought and hadn't seen her. As recognition grew, her eyes hardened. "Oh, it's you," she said flatly.

By now Raine wished she hadn't spoken. "Yes. How are you?" She tried again to put warmth in her voice.

"Do you really care?" Ann retorted.

Raine maintained her smile with difficulty. "Well, I—"

"Why did you have to come back?" Ann demanded harshly. "Why couldn't you have just stayed where you were and let everyone here…" She stopped herself, glancing at the customers going in and out of the grocery store. In deference to them she lowered her voice. "Don't think people haven't guessed why you did it. It's as plain as the nose on your face. People around here like Gabe. Respect him. They're really upset at the idea of someone like you using him.''

''Like me?'' Raine echoed, bristling.

''You get yourself pregnant by one of your fancy men in New York, then expect—''

Raine's arms tightened on her grocery bag. ''What makes you think the baby isn't Gabe's?''

''He's too good a man to—''

''Good men don't have sex?'' Raine challenged. ''If he asked, you wouldn't go to bed with him?''

''What makes you think I haven't already?'' Ann retorted.

For some reason the idea hurt. Raine had teased Gabe about his interest in other women. She'd wondered privately if he had a special girlfriend in Tyler or any of the surrounding towns. But the thought that it might be Ann Tully stung.

''You don't like that a bit, do you?'' the woman continued, and even though she smiled, her face was no longer pretty. ''Just think how *I* feel.'' And with that she disappeared into the store.

Raine slowly became aware that she was drawing curious looks. Elise Fairmont, the town's head librarian, changed direction in order to come speak to her—undoubtedly to offer some warm wishes. But Raine couldn't stand the idea of either more kindness or more reproach. All she wanted was the relative safety of home.

She turned without speaking and hurried away.

CHAPTER TEN

SOMETHING WAS WRONG again and Gabe didn't know what. From the time Raine had gotten up that morning she'd been quieter than usual, at first speaking only when answering a direct question, then later, speaking voluntarily but not often.

Was she ill? he wondered. Or was it the pregnancy? Either way, he wished she'd talk about it. When he'd pressed, she'd snapped at him. And from that point on, he had tried to stay mostly out of the way, using yard work as an excuse.

Yet all the time he was working outside, he worried about her. He'd give her another week, he decided, then he was going to see to it that she made an appointment with Hank Merton. It was important for an expectant mother to be under a doctor's care.

"Gabe, hello," Marge called to him as she crossed through the hedge separating the yards. "You're busy today. If George hadn't needed to see a patient this afternoon, I'd have pestered him until he came out and joined you. Our yard will be put to shame!"

"I didn't mean to do that," Gabe murmured, grinning.

Marge put her hands on her hips and looked around. "Your dad would be pleased. He always was particular about his yard. Where is he now? Have you heard from him lately?"

"When he called last week he was in South Dakota. Yesterday we got a postcard saying he'd crossed into Wyoming, on his way to Yellowstone Park. He could be there by now, I guess."

Marge tilted her head. "Still not planning to tell him yet?"

"Not for a while. What good would it do?"

"Not a lot, I suppose." She sighed.

Gabe's smile broadened. "Did you hear what the guys at the station did? Threw us a surprise party yesterday and gave us a present."

Marge didn't smile with him. "That was nice of them."

"Yeah," Gabe said. He glanced at Marge, then away again. Sometimes he forgot. Sometimes he could let himself fantasize that the marriage was real and that all the hoopla surrounding it had a purpose and wasn't just an exercise in futility.

"Don't let things get too out of hand, Gabe," Marge said soberly. "If you do, it will only be harder at the end."

"I'm not doing anything, Marge."

Her gaze remained steady. "You know what I mean."

Gabe moved uncomfortably. Had Marge, like his father, guessed his secret?

"I know why you're doing it," she continued. "To help Raine. But you have to protect yourself. You're the one who's going to be living here afterward. Raine...Raine will be back in New York."

Gabe breathed a little easier. She hadn't guessed.

"I'm not trying to be overly harsh on her," Marge continued. "You know me better than that. I love my daughter more than life itself. But I care for you, too, Gabe. And I don't want—''

He stopped her. ''I'm a big boy, Marge. I can take care of myself.''

A strange look passed over Marge's face—almost a dawning suspicion—then she shook her head and glanced toward his house. ''Is Raine at home?''

''She's there,'' he said. ''Only she's a little touchy at the moment.''

''I'll take care,'' Marge promised and went to the door.

RAINE STRAIGHTENED from closing the oven. Gabe hadn't been inside for more than an hour and she'd had time to make the stuffing, insert it in the bird and do most of the cleaning up. He had no idea that she was preparing their evening meal.

The familiar series of taps sounded on the back door and Raine went to answer it.

''Hi, Mom,'' she said, trying to sound chipper.

Her mother sniffed the air. ''Do I smell sage?'' she asked.

''You certainly do. I'm making stuffed chicken. I just put it in to bake.''

''Gabe says you're out of sorts.''

''I was…but I'm better now.''

''Anything in particular the cause?'' Marge made herself at home by sitting at the table.

''No,'' she claimed as she went to finish with the washing up, but she knew her mother wasn't deceived.

''Now why don't I believe that?'' Marge murmured.

''Would you and George like to come over for

dinner tonight?'' Raine asked. ''We're going to have plenty.''

''It's our bridge night. Raine, I can tell when something is wrong.''

Raine positioned the last bowl in the drying rack, then turned to face her mother. ''What did you come over here for, Mom?'' she asked.

''To see you. Do I have to have a special reason?''

''No.''

''Then?''

Raine sighed. ''I'm perfectly all right, if that's what you're worried about. I'm fine, the baby's fine—''

''What you need,'' her mother interrupted, ''is a good, old-fashioned shopping trip. Nothing like it to pick up the spirits. Not for maternity things…you don't need them yet. But some new clothes that will be comfortable over the next couple of months. What do you say?''

''Now? I can't—''

''How about tomorrow? Say one o'clock? We never managed to have many shopping trips together when you were growing up, did we? I was always so busy at the diner. You had to do almost everything for yourself.''

''It made me independent.''

''Maybe too independent.''

''One o'clock sounds great,'' Raine confirmed.

Marge smiled, the first real smile Raine had seen her give since she'd come into the house. ''I fought George tooth and nail about giving up control of the diner. But he kept telling me that life is so precious we shouldn't waste it. We're both relatively young. There're so many things we can do…and he was right. Now we have the best of both worlds—him with a few private patients, me going in to the diner only when I want. It's wonderful! And it's especially wonderful when you and I can... I wish you wouldn't go back to New York, Raine.'' The confession spilled out. ''It's so far away, and with the baby...''

Raine's eyelids fluttered.

Her mother rushed on, as if an idea had just occurred to her and she was pulling it together as she spoke. ''You could find something to do here. Maeve Kellaway, Cecil's niece, moved to California, and since she's gone, there's been no one to teach dancing to the little kids. You could do that. Tyler's had a baby boom in the past few years. You'd have plenty of work!''

''What about Gabe?'' Raine asked.

''What about him?'' her mother replied, but Raine could tell from the way she said it that she was fully aware of the difficulty. Finally she sighed deeply and muttered, ''And I just warned *him* to be careful.''

Raine frowned. ''You warned him? What about?''

''About letting things get too far out of hand... about expectations exceeding reality.''

''Whose expectations?''

Marge waved a hand. ''Everyone in town! I knew about the collection for the trip, but I couldn't do anything about it. I couldn't say 'no, don't.' And the talk. It's dying down a bit now, I think, but not in some quarters. But then in those quarters, it will never die down. They'll be talking about it for years to come. Especially if you and Gabe separate.''

''And I'll be judged the villainess,'' Raine murmured. ''Appropriate.''

''No. It's not appropriate. You aren't bad.''

"Some people think I am. Ann Tully told me yesterday that I shouldn't have come back to Tyler. And Richard Jensen—"

"Gabe's good friend? He was nasty to you?"

"No, just protective of Gabe. Like a lot of people."

Her mother sat back. "I wish I knew what to tell you."

"You can't tell me anything, Mom. I'm the one who made the decision. Except…"

"Except what?" Marge prompted.

Raine made a show of straightening the salt and pepper shakers in their wire tray. "Are Gabe and Ann Tully seeing each other? I mean…were they?"

"As boyfriend and girlfriend? Or rather, *woman* friend in this case. She's thirty-eight. I know that for a fact."

Raine nodded.

Her mother's forehead puckered. "I don't believe so. I've never heard anyone say anything. But then, I've been away from the diner so much lately. Is that something you've heard?"

"Sort of."

"It's possible, I suppose. Gabe is a very attractive man. A lot of women would like to get his attention. He helps out with her son a lot, doesn't he?"

Raine nodded again.

Marge shrugged. "Then it's possible, I suppose. What's it called—serendipity? The good fortune of being in the right place at the right time? Something like that, anyway."

"Something like that," Raine agreed. Now she felt worse than she had before. She had wanted her mother to disagree immediately. To tell her that there

could be no intimate association between Gabe and
Ann. But her hopes had been squashed.

Her mother looked at her closely. "Would it matter if..." She let the question dangle.

Raine shook her head quickly. "No. No, of course
not. I was just curious, that's all."

Marge didn't say anything for a moment, then she
stood up. "I'd better be getting back. George said he
wouldn't be long. And tomorrow we'll shop...
right?"

"I'll be over at your house at one," Raine promised, standing up as well.

Her mother kissed her cheek, smiled encouragement, then left the house. As she crossed through the
hedge she waved to Gabe.

Raine stood at the open door. She pretended to
watch her mother, but instead she watched Gabe. He
was trimming the hedge with an elderly set of hedge
clippers—his elbows extended, the muscles in his
back working with each short, chopping movement.
Muscles that were well defined by his sweat-
dampened white T-shirt. For several seconds Raine
couldn't pull her gaze away, then very quickly, as if
suddenly burned, she backed out of the way of the
door and closed it.

"YOU MADE DINNER?" Gabe said, surprised when he
came inside the house later.

"I'm not completely useless." Raine busied herself setting the table so she wouldn't have to look at
him. He'd brought scents of the outdoors with him—
tilled earth, freshly cut greenery, honest toil.

"I never thought you were," he replied.

"Well, I'm not," she sparred, for some reason

feeling more comfortable being irritated with him than not.

Gabe rubbed the back of his neck and allowed a tiny smile. "Stuffed chicken, if my nose remembers right."

"It is."

"What's the occasion?"

She flashed him a short look. "Just…dinner. Are you going to take a shower?"

His smile broadened. "I planned to."

"Good. The chicken needs to bake longer."

She bustled about the kitchen, a grown-up version of the mommy she'd once played in that silly game. But instead of running off at first opportunity, as he used to, Gabe stayed to watch her. Finally, pushed to the brink by his continued dawdling, she demanded, "What are you doing?"

"Remembering," he said softly.

Raine's displeasure melted away. He had a knack for saying the right thing at the right time…and meaning it. But instinct told her it was vitally important that she not let go completely. "Just—just go take your shower, okay?" she directed instead.

Gabe's blue gaze never wavered. Then, as if bowing to a force he found unfathomable, he left the room.

RAINE FELT even more unsettled during the meal. It had turned out beautifully—the chicken tender, the stuffing seasoned just right, the mashed potatoes without a single lump, the fresh green beans still slightly crisp. Gabe ate with uninhibited enjoyment.

"That was wonderful," he said afterward. "You should be giving me pointers."

"I can only cook a few things. Most of the time I eat out. At least, I used to."

"We can go out," Gabe offered.

She shook her head. "It's different here."

Gabe studied his empty plate. A moment later he surprised her by asking, "Are you that unhappy here, Raine? Is that why…"

Raine knew why he'd stopped. His reference was to her earlier behavior, and he'd hesitated to proceed. She hated that he felt that way. She hated that she had given him cause. She wasn't unhappy here. It was… She didn't know what it was! Except everything was becoming so topsy-turvy, so inside out! She tried to make her answer truthful.

"I'm not unhappy," she said.

"Then let's try the reverse. Are you happy?"

Raine protested. "That's not a fair question, Gabe. Under the circumstances—"

"Is it because you think *I'm* unhappy that you're upset? I've told you before, I know what I'm doing."

"I'm not upset!" she claimed. "I…" She stopped herself.

"You what?"

She leaned forward. "Gabe, you have a very full life here. You have a job, close friends. There must be someone special! A girlfriend…*several* girlfriends. And yet—"

"No one who's special, Raine."

"Not even Ann Tully?"

Gabe became very still. "Why do you ask that?"

"She's pretty, you help her son. It would only be natural if… And there wouldn't be anything wrong with it. You were free, she was…well, as good as free."

"Has she said something to you?" he asked shortly.

Raine didn't want to tell him word for word what had been said. "I just...wondered," she said evasively.

"I told you Ann has a lot of problems right now. She's very vulnerable. Anyone who's nice to her—"

"You're not just anyone, Gabe. Like Britt said the other night, you're a guardian angel. To me, to other people."

"That's a lot of rot."

"No, it's not." She scooted her chair closer to his and captured his hand. "How many other men would have done what you did for me? You're special, Gabe. Very special, and everyone knows it."

Gabe tried to withdraw his hand, but Raine wouldn't let go.

"Joel wouldn't, that's for sure," she said, forgetting for the moment that she had never told Gabe his name. "He only thinks about himself. What he wants, what he needs. He says and does the most outrageous things and people are fascinated. The first time we met...I'd never seen anyone like him!"

"You like men to be selfish?" Gabe's voice was oddly rough.

"No. At least... It was everything about him! His talent, his ability, his celebrity. The air vibrates when he comes into a room. I'm not the only one who feels it! And when he looked at me, I—"

The legs of Gabe's chair scraped against the floor, startling her.

"That's enough!" he said tightly, rising to his feet. "I don't want to hear any more. I wish you hadn't even said his name!"

Raine stood as well, but slowly. Gabe was angry. Why? "Gabe, I—"

A spasm moved like a lightning flash across his features. And before she knew what was happening, he had grabbed her, wound his fingers through her hair and brought her face up to his.

His lips bore down on hers, almost hurting her, then in an instant they softened—the kiss turning into a perfect blending of sweetness and sensuality that seemed to go on and on.

Raine was in shock. This was Gabe—*Gabe!*— kissing her like... This wasn't a brotherly kiss!

The kiss hardened again...then it was over, and she was set free. She caught hold of the nearest chair, her emotions in an uproar. She didn't know what to say, what to do, how to act. There was no coherent activity in her brain to guide her. It was all she could do to remain standing.

Gabe moved away from her, obviously just as shaken as she was. "I—" He choked and could go no further.

Raine slid back into the chair. Her heart was thundering, her breath almost nonexistent. She tried to speak but couldn't. Neither could she meet his gaze.

"Raine..." Her name fell into the strained silence, a strangled plea. "I don't know... I can't... What happened..."

GABE BROKE OFF his stumbling attempts to excuse his actions. As he watched her sitting there so quietly, so disturbed, he cursed himself for his lapse of control. The one thing they'd had going between them—from childhood!—was trust. A trust he'd just breached.

It didn't matter that he loved her. That hearing her talk about her lover, *Joel,* had torn him apart inside. Hearing her say how she felt when Joel looked at her...

He shook his head impatiently. Flagellating himself further wouldn't help. Nor would remembering how sweet her lips had tasted, far sweeter than he'd imagined.

He needed to make amends, to repair the fabric of their friendship. But how to explain? What to say?

He ran a hand through his short hair, then did so again. His limbs were trembling lightly, from an excess of need and fear. He didn't want to lose her!

He moved carefully back to her side. When she jumped at his nearness, a searing pain tore through his heart.

"Raine," he said softly, repentantly. "Red...I don't know what happened just now. I don't know why I..." He stopped to swallow. "All I can promise is that it won't happen again. You don't have to worry. We made an arrangement when we entered into this marriage and I won't... It *won't* happen again."

Raine finally looked at him. Her expression was so vulnerable, her eyes so confused. He wanted to pull her to him, just to hold her until everything was better, but at the moment that was the worst thing he could do. He didn't like being in that position. But he had no one else to blame except himself. He held his breath, waiting for her to speak.

"I believe you," she said softly, almost as if she were caught in a dream.

Then she got up and, without looking at him again, left the kitchen.

RAINE WALKED down the hall and turned into the bedroom, then closed the door, sealing herself inside. She might have been Alice in Wonderland, fallen down the rabbit's hole. She still hadn't gotten over the shock.

Gabe had kissed her. With passion. As a man kisses a woman he desires.

She crossed to the bed and sat down on the edge, her knees together, her hands folded in her lap.

He'd kissed her.

And she'd enjoyed it.

WHEN SHE LEFT the bedroom an hour later it was to find the dishes done and herself alone in the house. This time there was no note. Because Gabe didn't know what to say?

In a way she was relieved to be alone, in another she wasn't. She'd spent the past hour trying to sort through her thoughts, but it had done little good.

Gabe had always held the highest place of friendship in her heart. Good, steady, dependable Gabe. Always there for her, a solid presence. She'd accepted his solicitude without question, almost without thought. He would always be there for her and she for him.

She for him... Just how many times over the years had she aided him? Wasn't it almost entirely the other way around? Even as a childhood companion he'd had less need. He was the one who helped her. As if he'd been appointed.

Gabe...the child, the young man, the adult. She valued him in her life.

She remembered his kiss, the way surprise had been overtaken by a surge of feeling. She doubted that he'd picked up on it, because in her frozen state even she couldn't believe what was happening to her. But a thaw had definitely set in…and it was this that unsettled her most of all.

She was physically attracted to *Gabe?*

CHAPTER ELEVEN

WHEN RAINE SAW Gabe the next morning he behaved as if nothing out of the ordinary had passed between them. She took her cue from him. They talked about the weather, the fact that Mr. Foster had called again, Gabe's upcoming birthday…anything but the kiss.

It was obvious that the episode was never far from either of their minds, though. It was there in the careful way each moved when the other was nearby. In the fleeting looks and the pauses in speech.

The atmosphere was highly uncomfortable, and as soon as he could Gabe escaped.

"I'm going to see Mr. Foster," he said, "then I have to talk to Reverend Sarah, then—" he looked from Raine to the door "—then there are some other things."

"Of course," Raine murmured. She understood perfectly. If she hadn't had a shopping trip planned with her mother, she would have invented one in order to get away herself! "Remember, I'll probably be with Mom for most of the afternoon, so if you come back early…"

"I'll know where you are."

Raine hated the strain that had sprung up between them. She wanted things to be as they used to be.

Herself and Gabe, the best of friends. Free and easy, companionable. Able to hold each other and not—

She pulled her gaze away from his before he could sense what she was thinking: *and not have it turn into something else.*

She heard Gabe go out the door, and once she was alone, she released a long breath.

THE SHOPPING TRIP turned out to be far more enjoyable than Raine had expected. She and her mother had fun sharing unaccustomed moments. It was almost as if both were trying to make up for the past. For the first time they were able to come together as friends as well as mother and daughter. They drove to the mall in Sugar Creek, strolled from store to store, had an afternoon snack at a little pastry shop that Marge knew, before returning to Tyler and Gates Department Store.

"If we see Nora, don't tell her we went to the mall," Marge advised as she parked her car. "I always feel so disloyal, even though I know she knows that everyone does it."

Raine shook her head and smiled. "She runs a business, Mom, just like you do. You don't get upset when people eat at the lodge, do you? Or even at the Dairy King?"

"Well, no…"

"Same thing."

"Still, it was so nice of her to help me with my make-over."

"She likes you. She probably enjoyed it."

Marge laughed. "I do sometimes catch her looking at me with a satisfied little smile. I'm almost afraid to go into Byron's art gallery. He's the one who took the photos of me, you know. The before and after. I'm afraid I might find images of myself up on the wall next to some of Renata Youngthunder's work!''

"That would be a compliment," Raine assured her.

"It would scare me half to death! I'd rather not know!''

The minute they stepped through the entrance of the department store a wealth of memories flooded over Raine. She had forgotten how beautiful the interior was and how straight out of another era, with its wood-and-glass display cases, Tiffany ceilings and sweeping staircase that led to the floors above. Good service and quality were the store's hallmark. As was the still-operating glass-and-brass pneumatic tube system that sent money and receipts back and forth to the accounting department. Gates Department Store had been a fixture in Tyler since the early 1920s, opened by Nora's namesake and great-aunt, Eleanora Gates, now deceased.

Up to this point in the shopping trip Raine had avoided spending a great deal of money by finding fault with many of the things that they'd seen. But that didn't wash here. Nora and her buyer had excellent taste and offered a wide selection of quality merchandise.

"Try this on," her mother urged, pulling a dress from a rack. "Oh, these colors will be so pretty on you! This could take you almost all the way through. The material's so soft and the cut so loose."

Raine surreptitiously looked at the price tag. She winced to herself. "I only need a couple of dresses, Mom. And we already have those. If anything, I need more pants."

Her mother frowned. "But this dress is so pretty! Try it on at least. Just to see. For me?"

Nora Gates Forrester spotted them as Raine modeled the dress for her mother in front of a long mirror. "It looks like it was made for you, Raine," she said, coming over to greet them. "The yellow and rust tones are perfect with your coloring."

Raine shrugged. The other two women gazed at her reflection. "I don't think I—" She was about to refuse when her mother interrupted her.

"Let me buy it for you," Marge suggested, having guessed the problem.

Raine shook her head.

"But it's so pretty on you, dear," her mother cajoled.

Nora said, "If you don't have enough cash with you, Raine, you can always put it on Gabe's account. He has one with the store, you know."

Raine hadn't known.

Nora smiled. "If he saw you in that, I'm certain he'd agree. You like it, don't you?"

"Yes," Raine answered honestly.

"Then let me put it on his account."

"You could wear it for his birthday!" her mother suggested.

"Gabe's birthday?" Nora questioned.

"It's the eighteenth. This Saturday," Marge said.

"Are you going to have a party for him?" Nora asked.

Raine's attention had been bouncing back and forth between the two women. She was slightly startled when both of them looked at her and waited for an answer. "I, ah, I don't know," she said.

"Well, if you do, we've just gotten in some of the nicest party notions. They're on the third floor."

"I, ah, I'll have to think about it," Raine mumbled, and escaped back into the changing room.

Her mother was still looking at dresses when Raine returned, the yellow-and-rust dress hanging over her arm. "You win," she said when Marge looked up. "I'm buying it."

Money was something she and Gabe had not yet discussed, and the subject had been neglected long enough. She had a good five months before the baby would make working too difficult. She couldn't just continue to do nothing. Her mother's idea of teaching little children the basics of dance was starting to appeal…as strange as that idea might sound to some of her friends in New York.

They shopped in the department store for another half hour, Raine splurging on several pairs of stretch slacks and a couple of loose-fitting blouses.

Outside, as they walked down the sidewalk, Raine's purchases folded in a distinctive Gates Department Store shopping bag, her mother once again brought up the idea of a thirtieth birthday party for Gabe. "It would be nice," she said. "It would make him feel appreciated."

The muscles in Raine's stomach tightened.

"It wouldn't have to be big," Marge continued, "just a few friends." She glanced at her daughter.

The pressure mounted. How could she refuse? "Sure," Raine said. "I think he's off duty on Saturday. I'll have to check."

"Marge!" someone called from across the street. "Marge, Raine…wait!"

Raine and her mother stopped walking as Elise

Fairmont, smiling and waving, made her way across the street from the square.

Raine looked away for a second, ashamed of the way she'd run from the other woman outside the grocery store. But she'd just had her confrontation with Ann Tully and hadn't felt comfortable facing anyone else, not even the gentle librarian.

Little about Elise's outward appearance had changed over the years. She must be in her late fifties by now, Raine thought, but she was one of those tall, naturally thin women who look very much the same all their lives. Her pale blond hair, worn short and lightly curled, was streaked with silver, but the colors blended so perfectly that it was hard to tell. She had nice skin and soft blue eyes. Yet it was inside that the change had occurred. Where before she'd been a little too quiet and serious, she now smiled freely and moved with confidence.

"Marge! Raine!" she cried, clasping their hands. "I just couldn't let this moment slip by. I looked up and there you were…and I had to stop you. Raine," she said, "I'm so pleased you're back in Tyler. You always did brighten up the place. Especially the library, when you used to stop by in your dance costumes on the way to practice or a recital."

Raine smiled. "I was usually late with a book report or a paper at school and had been threatened with a trip to Miss Mackie's office if I didn't get it in the next day."

"Josephine ran a tight ship," Elise said. "Have you heard that she's off on a cruise to the Greek islands? She tried to talk Robert and me into going with her, but Robert couldn't get away. He's still teaching at the university."

Raine had never met Robert Fairmont, but when Elise had married him four years previously, her mother had written an unusually long letter, telling Raine all about it. Raine knew that he was an architect and that because of him both Elise and her older sister, Bea, had broken out of the years-long inertia surrounding them.

Bea had never been one of Raine's favorite people. While Raine was growing up, Bea had been grouchy and mean to any child who made noise outside the house she then shared with Elise. *And* she'd call their parents to complain.

Almost as if Elise had read Raine's mind, she said, "So we talked Bea into going instead! Which wasn't all that difficult, it turned out, since she's always had a secret desire to go there!"

Raine was trying to formulate an appropriate response when a commotion started a little farther down the sidewalk. A woman with her hair set partially in curlers came running out of Tisha Olsen's beauty salon, yelling for help. Another woman—this one with a clear plastic bag tied over her wet, purple-tinted hair—came hurrying onto the sidewalk after her. "Hurry!" she cried, ringing her hands. "Please help us! Please!"

Everyone in the vicinity froze. Then the first woman came running back, with a man hard on her heels—Gabe! He disappeared into the shop after her.

A crowd began to gather outside the Hair Affair, and Raine, her mother and Elise Fairmont were close to the front. Raine watched through the large plate-glass window as several women, including the two who had run outside, hovered in the background while Gabe bent over a redheaded woman collapsed on the floor. Another woman, obviously a beautician because she wore a bright pink operator's smock with several combs sticking out of a pocket, stood off to the other side.

"What's the matter? What's happened?" newcomers to the crowd asked excitedly.

"It's Tisha," Elise breathed.

"What's wrong with her? Did anyone say?"

"Is that her on the floor?" a man demanded, craning his neck to see.

Gabe was working on Tisha, running through a medical procedure he'd obviously been trained to employ. The operator, upon his instruction, hurried to the telephone. But someone else must have already placed a call for help because the wail of a siren could be heard in the distance.

As it drew nearer, everyone held their breath.

"Is she dead?" someone asked in a hushed tone.

"Gabe's in there," a woman stated, seeming confident that his presence could chase away any evil. His name reverberated through the crowd.

The siren screamed as the ambulance made a quick turn onto Main Street. When Raine looked around she saw the technicians hop out and start to clear a path to the beauty salon's entrance. She, her mother and Elise, among others, pressed together to make way.

The technicians hurried past. One spoke to Gabe, while the other bent over Tisha, whom Raine saw move her arm.

"She moved her arm," she said to her mother. Other people heard, and there was a tentative sigh of relief.

"Someone should call Judson," Elise said.

"Maybe Jeff first," Marge suggested, "so he can break the news gently to his grandfather. Judson and Tisha just came back from Arizona for the summer, didn't they?"

"A few days ago," Elise confirmed.

"I'll make the call," Marge volunteered.

"I'll come with you," Elise murmured, and the two women hurried away.

Raine couldn't make herself go with them. She watched as Gabe stood aside as the two technicians worked. Then she saw him help transfer Tisha onto a rolling stretcher and assist as they took her out the front door to the street.

Once again the crowd parted, silently witnessing the event.

Within seconds Tisha was placed inside the rescue vehicle, one technician jumping into the back with her, while the other—the driver—secured the rear doors. Before getting behind the wheel, though, he thanked Gabe and clapped him on the shoulder.

Gabe stood back with the crowd as the ambulance pulled away, its siren once again screaming.

"What was wrong with her, Gabe?" someone asked. "Was it serious?"

Gabe shook his head. "Can't tell. She'll have to have some tests."

"Was it her heart?" another person asked.

"Oh, I was so frightened!" The woman with the wet purple hair dissolved into tears. "I thought—I thought she was *dead!*"

"Me, too!" the first woman said. "She was so pale, and then she just collapsed. She was doing my hair...like she always does when she's in town. We were talking, then she stopped, looked kind of funny, made a little noise and fell. Oh, it was horrible! *Horrible!*"

Gabe made his way unerringly to Raine. He grasped her hand and pulled her away from the crowd, ducking into the drugstore nearby.

Raine's throat was so tight she couldn't speak. Thoughts and emotions overwhelmed her. The way Gabe had rushed into the shop, the way he had ministered to Tisha, the faith of the people outside that he could take care of the problem…it all mingled with her own confused feelings for him. He was the Gabe she had always known and yet he wasn't. He was much more.

"Tisha?" she croaked.

"It could be her heart."

"Is it bad?" she asked tightly.

"I've seen worse. But there's no way to know until the doctors check her out."

"What were you… How…?"

"I was on my way to the hardware store. One of the ladies saw me and called me over."

Raine knew that her reaction was all out of proportion to the past moments. It wasn't as if the sudden affliction had struck someone she loved. She knew Tisha Olsen and had always admired her for her sometimes outrageous personality and sense of humor. But that was as far as it went. They weren't particularly close.

Gabe frowned and touched her arm. His hand was warm and strong. She trembled.

"This isn't doing you any good," he said.

Raine looked around, suddenly realizing that when her mother returned she would have no idea what had happened to her. "Mom was here. She'll be looking for me...."

The crowd had dispersed by the time Raine and Gabe went back outside. Only a few people remained to discuss the event.

"Raine! There you are!" Marge cried, breaking away from a small group. "I wondered where you went. But I thought if Gabe didn't have to go to the hospital, you'd be with him. Hello, Gabe." Marge's features were strained, as if the experience had been difficult for her as well. But then she and Tisha were closer in age and in friendship. "I called Jeff Baron," she said to Gabe, "so he could alert his grandfather. It took forever! He was in some kind of meeting, but I finally got through."

"I think Raine should go home now, Marge," Gabe said.

As Marge turned to examine her closely, Raine could see the worry start to grow in her mother's eyes. Now that her mother was used to the idea of her being pregnant, she didn't want anything to cause Raine to lose the baby.

"I'm all right, really," Raine said, trying to re-assure her. Trying to reassure Gabe.

"My car's right here," Marge said, motioning to the late-model Lincoln parked in an angled slot. "We were going home anyway. We'd just finished our shopping for the day."

Gabe hesitated.

"It's all right," Marge assured him. "If you're in the middle of something, I'll look after her. This is my grandbaby we're talking about, remember?"

Raine would have sworn she saw Gabe wince. He

covered it quickly if he had, though, and replied, "I was on my way to pick up something for someone."

"I'll see to her then," Marge said, and within a second she had hustled Raine into the car and was on her way around to the driver's side.

Gabe stood motionless on the sidewalk, his gaze fixed on Raine, as the Lincoln backed quickly out of the parking slot.

When it pulled away Raine felt as if a part of herself had been left behind.

RAINE HADN'T planned on going to sleep. Her mother had insisted that she lie down, and after a heated protest, she had. A couple of hours later she awakened to find that her mother had gone and Gabe was in the kitchen, stirring something on the stove.

"I didn't mean to go to sleep," she said, running a hand over her tousled hair.

"You needed it."

She slumped into a chair. "Have you heard how Tisha is?"

"I called the hospital about a half hour ago. They said she's resting comfortably."

"Is that all they can say?"

"That's a lot. At least she's stabilized." He glanced at her. "The stew's going to be a while. Do you want something to tide you over?"

Raine shook her head.

There was a moment of silence.

"Did you find what you wanted on your shopping trip?" he asked.

Raine stirred. The shopping trip seemed to have happened a very long time ago. "More than I meant to, actually. Gabe, I put some clothes on your account at Nora's store. She said you had one.''

Gabe looked pained. ''I should have given you my card. Sorry.''

''No, it's not that. I only wanted you to know about the charges, so when the bill comes in you'll be expecting it.''

''Not a problem,'' he said.

She lifted her chin. ''I plan to pay for everything myself. You've already done enough. I don't want you paying my debts as well. I may have to borrow a bit at first, but I'll pay you back. You know that.''

''I'm not interested in the money, Raine.''

''I have to do this, Gabe. For me. Mom gave me an idea. I'm not sure if it'll work, but she said Mrs. Kellaway moved to California and there's no one here to take her place teaching dance to little kids. I could do that.''

''You could,'' Gabe agreed.

She frowned. ''I'm not sure how to start.''

''Talk to Angela Murphy. She opened TylerTots a few years ago. It started small and grew, and now it's quite a successful business.''

His automatic assumption that she was ready to make such long-term plans rattled Raine. She moved restlessly to the kitchen window. Once again the day was sunny and warm. More and more plants were bursting into leaf and bloom.

She swung around, turning her back on the springtime frivolities. Would it be fair for her to start something with the children that she might not be around to finish? To expose them to the initial joys of dance, only to take it away when it was no longer convenient to her plans?

"Then again," she said tightly, reacting to the conflict inside her, "maybe I won't."

Gabe didn't move.

"It wouldn't be fair, Gabe," she continued, speaking her thoughts aloud. "I don't know how long I'm going to be here, or if I'll want to teach after the baby's born." She sighed, frustrated. "There are just too many things to consider. I'll have to think about it."

"Thinking's good," Gabe said evenly.

Raine shot him an irritated look. "Don't agree with everything I say, please!"

Gabe held her gaze for a long moment. Then, lips tightening, he adjusted his grasp on the stirring spoon, walked over to her, folded it into her hand and went out the door.

A flash of anger erupted in Raine as she stood there with the unwanted spoon. How dared he just leave like that! His normally amiable face had been set in stone, his blue eyes, always so warm with care and humor, frosty. He was angry with her. Why? What had she…? Raine took a series of short breaths and tried to see it from his perspective. Maybe she was lucky that he was a man of such control. Another man might have yelled and made her feel much worse than she already did.

Raine slumped back into the chair. She had to face it. Her uncalled-for outburst had not been about her need for money or the frustration involved in finding a way to get it. She had railed at Gabe because he was the source of so much of her trouble. Even if he didn't know it!

GABE STORMED outside, taking his anger and frustration out by tossing a few lay-up shots into the basket hanging from the backboard at the front of the garage. When he made those, he switched to longer shots, dribbling the ball in between, pounding it on the pavement. The twanging *ka-thump* as the ball hit the rim, whether it went in or not, was satisfying.

He didn't know whether he was angry at her or at himself. She was being wholly unreasonable, but he didn't seem to have very much patience anymore, either. Why not?

When he'd entered into this arrangement he'd known that it was going to be difficult living in the same house with Raine, dealing with her day after day. Wanting her and yet not being able to show it.

Then he'd slipped up and kissed her.

Idiot! he swore, pounding the ball on the pavement all the harder.

He wanted everything between them to be as it had been before, but that didn't look as if it was going to happen.

Which meant that their possible future together was even more at risk.

He pounded the ball a few more times, before sending it rolling into the garage. Then he hopped in the Explorer and backed out of the drive. Once again he had to get away.

THE RHYTHMIC THUMP of the basketball ceased. Raine noted the absence of sound and looked out the window. She was just in time to see Gabe drive away.

She wanted to run after him and apologize. But he was out of sight before she could even move. In all probability he was going off somewhere to help someone in his precious town, she thought acidly. Maybe Ann Tully.

She groaned out loud at the thought. And if it wasn't Ann Tully, it could be someone else. He had a full life here. And a full life meant that it was *full*. A man as nice looking and reputable as Gabe probably had to beat women off with a stick! He was a fire fighter, for glory's sake! He wore a uniform! He had a sweet, shy smile that many women must find irresistible.

Raine started to pace, then she stopped. She'd bought some nice things today. She was going to go try them on. And she wasn't going to think about Gabe!

Raine was trying on a second dress when she smelled something burning. The stew! She raced out of the bedroom and down the hall. Smoke rose in soft billows from the pot, collecting in the higher corners of the kitchen. She'd forgotten it was cooking!

Screeching, she carried the pot outside and abandoned it on top of a metal garbage can, then she hurried back inside to open all the windows and doors. She remembered the other poor soul Gabe had told her about who had forgotten his snack on the burner. A fire engine had rolled up, embarrassing him greatly. She didn't want the same thing to happen to her. Or for Gabe to hear about it later—which he would, without doubt.

She ran through the house flapping her arms, trying to make the smoke dissipate as quickly as possible. It amazed her that the alarm in the hall hadn't gone off yet. But as bad as the situation seemed at first, the smoke quickly faded, and a liberal spraying of her best perfume helped cover the smell.

She changed out of her new dress and back into the clothes she had worn all day. When Gabe returned a half hour later, she saw him pause and sniff the air. He had to have known what had happened, but he said nothing—not even when the meal they ate for dinner that evening came straight out of a can.

CHAPTER TWELVE

THE STRAIN between Raine and Gabe grew worse during Gabe's two remaining days off duty. They spoke, but not often and not about anything of great personal depth. They avoided touching. They avoided meeting each other's eyes.

When he wasn't leaving the house on some pretext, Raine was. She went out to Britt's farm then followed Britt back into town and was given a tour of the brand-new yogurt shop. Other times Raine just drove, letting the wind blow through the open windows and take her troubles away…at least for a short time.

That was why the birthday party was going to be such a farce. Gabe wasn't at all enthused, and she certainly wasn't looking forward to it. But when Saturday night rolled around, both were at the door, greeting guests—Raine with a smile plastered on her face and Gabe seemingly equally happy.

The day before, Raine had returned to Gates Department Store to shop for some of the party notions Nora had recommended, and probably because she wasn't enthusiastic, she'd gone a little overboard. The seldom-used dining-room table was awash with colorful plates, napkins, party hats, confetti and long curling ribbons. Helium balloons floated in the air. In the middle of the table was a professionally decorated cake. The entire motif was styled for an adult, but Raine had held her breath when Gabe first saw it. His eyes had widened, but he'd made no disparaging comment.

The guests were the same people who'd been at Marge's the week before, with the addition of Richard Jensen and the loss of Byron Forrester. Byron had a commitment he couldn't get out of, but he'd sent his best wishes along with Nora. Because most of the people were close friends, there was no awkwardness as the party-goers gathered. The night was taken in a spirit of fun, with gag gifts and much laughter. Even Richard seemed to enjoy himself, going so far as to don a party hat like everyone else.

"Now wasn't this a good idea?" Marge whispered to Raine as more laughter erupted from the living room. The two of them were in the kitchen preparing to serve coffee to the crowd, who'd earlier toasted Gabe's birthday with the champagne Marge and George had brought.

Raine's nerves were on edge, stretched even tighter by the strain of the party, yet she nodded. "Yes, it certainly was."

"Is there anything I can do to help?" Susannah Santori asked, stepping into the room.

Mother and daughter turned, almost in unison.

Raine forced another smile. "I think everything's under control. All we have to do is wait for the coffee to finish perking, which shouldn't be long."

Susannah settled in a chair. Beside her delicately made body, Raine felt positively huge. It was hard to gauge how old Susannah was. From everything Raine knew of her, she was probably in her forties, but she could have passed for a woman half that age.

"I can't tell you the number of people who have mentioned the thank-you note you sent them, Raine," Susannah said. "Everyone was impressed with what you said."

Raine shrugged. "I didn't really say all that much."

"I appreciated it myself. It was sweet. You know, when I had my television show in Milwaukee, one of the things I always stressed was for people to be sure and send out thank-you notes. But you wouldn't believe the number who forget. Or feel it's too big a job. How did you do it so quickly?"

Raine had used the time she was alone in the house over the past few days. "It was probably due more to Annabelle Scanlon than to me. She must have rushed them through the mail."

"Speaking of Annabelle—" Susannah sat forward "—you and Gabe have been replaced as the prime topic of conversation, Raine. Now everyone's talking about Tisha. About how horrible it would have been *if...* Thank God it wasn't serious! A wake-up call, I've heard Jeff Baron called it."

"It frightened everyone to death," Marge murmured.

Susannah agreed. "Particularly Judson. I haven't seem him look so bad since his trial. I think he thought he was about to lose her."

"That's enough to scare anyone. I know if I were to lose George..." Marge didn't finish. Instead, she said, "But that's not going to happen now. Judson's not going to lose Tisha. She's getting out of the hospital tomorrow, isn't she?"

"I've heard that, too."

Raine straightened from arranging the tray. "It's

all ready,'' she said brightly, then lifting it, walked from the room. Her mother and Susannah followed closely.

To anyone who didn't know Gabe intimately, he seemed to be enjoying the party. He laughed and talked and poked fun with the others, but beneath the surface—revealed by the set of his shoulders and the way he held his head—he was tense, Raine could tell.

He met her eyes as she handed him his cup of coffee, and Raine almost bobbled it. No coffee spilled, though, so the incident passed unnoticed, except by Richard Jensen.

Raine felt his dark gaze follow her as she passed around the other cups. She pretended that it didn't bother her, but it did. From the first instant she'd met him she'd sensed that he could see far deeper into the situation than she wanted him to. Had he detected her growing confusion about Gabe?

She chose a chair out of his line of vision, but even then she felt vulnerable.

TO GABE'S RELIEF the party broke up shortly after eleven. He was concerned about Raine. She looked so stressed. That couldn't be good either for her or the baby. But there was nothing he could say or do to influence the situation. She was so sensitive at the moment that even a genial ''hello'' was enough to create a problem. She tightened up every time he came near her, as if…as if she didn't trust him. Didn't even *like* him anymore!

Marge stayed behind to help with the cleanup, and Gabe walked Nora to her car. When he returned it was to find Richard waiting for him just outside the kitchen door. His friend stood with his back to the garage, a foot propped against the wood siding. As Gabe drew nearer, Richard lit a cigarette.

"I thought you were going to give those up," Gabe said.

"Easier said than done."

Glasses clinked in the kitchen. Water ran in the sink. Raine and her mother were talking, but their words were muffled. Gabe wished that he could go inside, send Raine to bed and finish the job himself, but at present he doubted that his offer would be well received. He looked away from the window and unconsciously sighed.

"Nice party," Richard said.

"Yeah. Raine went a little overboard, though."

"Everyone enjoyed it."

"Yeah." Gabe bent to sweep a twig off the grass.

"Except you...and her."

Gabe broke the twig in half and tossed it away. "Yeah."

Richard took another draw on his cigarette. The smoke curled into the night air. "Things not going so well?" he asked after a moment.

Gabe was surprised by the sudden jolt of anger that overtook him. "Hell, I don't know," he exploded. "One minute you think you're doing the right thing, and the next...!"

"You sure it's not just growing pains? It takes a while to adjust in any marriage."

"What marriage?" Gabe snapped, then immediately wished that he hadn't.

Richard pushed away from the garage. "I'm your friend, right?" he asked.

"Right," Gabe answered tightly. He could feel his

colleague's deep concern, his desire to help. For Gabe, that was a unique situation. Not that he wasn't ever in need of help, but he was usually able to work most things out for himself. Except where it concerned Raine. For years his feelings for her had kept him off balance.

"Don't keep secrets," Richard said. "Whatever's the matter, get it out in the open. I'm the one who should know, remember?"

"This is a different situation," Gabe defended.

"It's two people trying to live under the same roof together, isn't it? Two people trying to get along?"

"This is *different!*"

"Does she know you love her?"

"No."

"Then tell her."

Gabe flared again. "It's not that easy!"

Richard bent down to stub out his cigarette before flicking it away. "Tell me about it," he drawled wryly. "Love can be as addicting as one of these."

WHEN GABE CAME into the house after Richard left, he and Raine glanced at each other, but neither said a word. Marge looked from one to the other.

"Did everyone get off all right?" she asked.

"Without a hitch," Gabe said.

Marge rinsed and dried her hands. "Well, that's everything done here. I suppose I'd better get myself over to my place. George will be waiting. Gabe, you're back on duty tomorrow morning, aren't you?"

"Seven a.m."

Marge grimaced. "Even more reason for me to get going." Yet she paused, directing another penetrating look at Raine. "Unless there's something else..."

Raine shook her head. She couldn't meet her mother's gaze or Marge would see the tears that hovered on her lashes. She was so tired, both physically and emotionally. The past few days had taken everything out of her. She felt bruised, drained.

The telephone rang and the sound made Raine jump. Her cheeks became stained with embarrassment as Gabe went to answer it.

Her mother continued to hover, only now she was frowning. "What is it, Raine? All evening I've felt... Have you and Gabe had an argument?"

"I don't want to talk about it, Mom. At least not right now."

"But Raine—"

"Later, Mom, okay?" Her hands curled tightly on the rim of the counter.

She could feel Marge's great need to ask more questions. Her mother was worried, because she loved her. But one thing Raine had learned over the past few weeks was that a parent's love, which could magically fix everything when you were young, could do little to repair grown-up problems. There came a point when a son or a daughter had to stand alone and deal with the slings and arrows of life.

"Okay," Marge agreed quietly and started for the door. But before going out she asked, "I'll see you tomorrow, right?"

Raine could only nod.

GABE SAT at the desk, his hand on top of the telephone. His father had called to wish him a happy birthday.

"It's far too late, I know," Charles Atwood had said, "but I got all mixed up in the time difference. I've moved out of Mountain Time into the Pacific time zone, and somehow I thought you'd be two hours earlier, rather than later. Anyway, happy birthday, son!"

He'd told Gabe all that he'd seen and a lot of what he'd done—things he couldn't fit on a postcard. He'd sounded relaxed and happy, and Gabe had hated to spoil his enjoyment of his vacation, but he'd decided earlier in the week that the next time his father called, he was going to tell him. It had reached the point where his father would be hurt if he didn't get the news soon.

His dad had reacted to the information with a long silence. Then he'd said, "I hope you know what you're doing, son."

Gabe had laughed, a little unsteadily. "I wouldn't have done it if I didn't, Dad."

"But a baby that's not yours! That's a lot to ask."

"She didn't ask. I did."

"But under the circumstances—"

"If it's all right with me, that's all that should matter, shouldn't it?" Gabe interrupted him.

His father was silent again. "You're certainly old enough to make your own decisions," he said finally. "I just hope—" He cut himself off, and Gabe heard his deep sigh. "I just hope everything works out. That you'll be happy. Both of you."

"There's no reason why we can't be."

Even though Gabe's bravado had fallen a little short, his father had gone on to tell him that since he was already in California, he was going to continue on to San Francisco before he started back.

Gabe had tried to talk him out of cutting his vacation short, telling him that there was no reason why he needed to return to Tyler, but Charles had been adamant. "I'm tired of living in a tin can, son."

There's no reason why we can't be happy. Gabe's claim echoed in his ears. It had sounded hollow because neither he nor Raine was happy now.

He heard a noise behind him and turned to see that she had started down the hall. His heart gave a funny little vibration.

"Raine?" he called after her quietly.

She braced her shoulders before she turned. "Yes?"

"That was my dad. I told him."

"Oh."

"He's coming home."

Her eyes darted down the hall toward the room she was borrowing.

Gabe smiled tightly. "He's going to see San Francisco first...dip a toe in the Pacific, he said...then he's turning back. It's going to take him a couple of weeks. He's like a snail, dragging his home behind him, remember? After that...well, I told you. We'll work something out. Everything's going to be just fine."

Her green eyes were luminous in the half-light. "Is it?" she whispered.

He stood up. *Don't keep secrets,* Richard had advised. But this was more than a secret. It was a land mine that could destroy everything.

She'd tensed even more. He could sense it even from this distance. For protection he ignored the question she'd posed. "And Raine?" he said instead. "It was a very nice party. Thank you."

Her eyes seemed to shimmer before she murmured something unintelligible and hurried down the hall.

RAINE CRIED silently in her room for she didn't know how long. She cried for herself, she cried for Gabe, she cried for this unknown tiny person who would make an appearance sometime during the middle of November. What did the future hold for any of them? Should she stay in Tyler, as her mother wanted, or should she leave? What would be best? For her, for the child, for Gabe?

She curled onto her side and looked at the photograph hanging on the wall. Positioned so that it could be easily seen from the bed, it was of a young woman, Gabe's mother, close to the age that her son was now. She had the same color hair and eyes. She was sitting on the hood of a car, leaning back on outspread arms, her chin up, her smile teasing.

Did she know? Could she, if she was in heaven, look down the road ahead and see what was in store for them? Ever since Raine had been using this bedroom, she'd stared at the photograph each night before going to sleep. Was that what Charles Atwood did? Immerse himself in the room that still held the essence of his wife and gaze upon her image, both before going to sleep and upon waking up?

Love. It was a funny emotion.

Raine had never been sure if her mother had loved her father. She'd never been able to penetrate the veil Marge had erected to defend herself against his betrayal. Raine assumed her mother once had loved him, but she didn't know for certain. As a child, she had only ever had a couple of photographs of him, and in both he'd been standing alone and staring at the camera with a go-ahead, give-me-your-best-shot swagger and grin.

But it was for sure that her mother loved George. The more Raine saw them together, the more apparent that became. It was a deep, comfortable kind of love with few surprises, but all the more secure because of that fact.

Love? In the past Raine had been in love with the idea of being in love. She'd thought herself in love several times. But it had never lasted, and truth to tell, she hadn't wanted it to. The feelings had always seemed hollow, somehow lacking.

The closest she'd come was with Joel.

Joel. She repeated the name in her mind, then tried it on her lips. It didn't have the same impact as it once had. Because he had rejected her? Was *she* wrapping herself in a veil of hurt, so she wouldn't have to think?

But she *did* feel!

In a sneak attack around her will, thoughts of Gabe arose. *Gabe!* And something within her spirit trembled, came to life.

No. It couldn't be! She couldn't be falling in love with Gabe! *No!*

Her gaze flew back to the woman who posed on the hood of the car, forever young, forever smiling. What did she know? Whom was she teasing?

Raine made a soft mew of distress and buried her face in her pillow.

She couldn't even let herself *think* about falling in love with Gabe!

GABE HAD BEEN at work for a full three hours by the time Raine awakened the next morning. Today there was no note, but at her place at the kitchen table she did find a leftover party hat and a scattering of confetti that he had left for her. Smiling faintly, she placed the hat on her head, then gathered the confetti and tossed it a little way into the air. ''Whee!'' she said in mock celebration.

As tired as she'd been last night, it had taken until the wee hours of the morning before she could fall aslccp. She had relived every minute she'd spent with Gabe since her return to Tyler, incident layered upon incident. She'd tried to remember every word they'd said.

She pulled the paper hat from her head and pushed it across the table. In the end, she still wasn't sure of anything. On one hand, it wasn't all that surprising that she might feel a special affection for the man who had offered himself as her champion. Who had a history of protecting her. On the other, her view of Gabe had never been anything but platonic...until now.

A short time later Raine went in search of her mother. As she had concluded last night, her mother's love would never be able to solve her problems for her, but it could offer comfort. Today Raine needed to be close to her, to hear her soothing voice.

She found her mother in the hobby room—Raine's old bedroom. Marge was sewing on another wall hanging.

''How's this for the new arrival?'' she asked, holding it up for Raine's inspection.

Raine smiled. Where the wall hanging for the Olsen baby had had the pertinent birth information embroidered inside colorful balloons, this one was in keeping with the newborn's Irish heritage. Large green shamrocks proclaimed the arrival of Brendan Pierce O'Conner, born on April 10 of that year and weighing in at a respectable seven pounds six ounces.

"That's wonderful, Mom!" Raine said. "What a great idea."

"I'm thinking that for our baby I'm going to use teddy bears, and if it's a girl, they'll be wearing frilly pink tutus."

"You're already planning that far ahead?"

"I can't help but think ahead. I'm going to enjoy being a grandmother, Raine."

Raine looked away. She wished that she could be as enthusiastic. That she could look ahead to the baby's birth with excitement and joy. But circumstances wouldn't let her. Not yet.

"What's the matter, honey?" her mother asked.

What *wasn't* the matter? Raine thought. She was tired of fighting everything. Tired of fighting herself. Tired of worrying about the future. Her placid outlook about her relationship with Gabe had received a severe jolt. She wasn't sure of anything anymore—which path to follow, or even if it was a viable route and not an illusion.

"Does it have something to do with Gabe?" Marge guessed when she didn't answer.

Raine bit her bottom lip and shook her head, denying it at the same time as her body language offered confirmation.

"I know something is wrong, Raine. I'm not being nosy, I'm trying to help. Has he said something, done something?"

Again Raine shook her head.

Marge made a frustrated movement.

"Mom…" Raine choked. "I'm not sure…" Her throat closed again, stopping her from going on.

Marge leaned forward to take her hands. "Not sure about what?" she prompted.

"He kissed me," Raine whispered tightly.

Marge became very still. "And?"

Raine shrugged. "That's it. He just…kissed me. But I wanted to kiss him back!"

Marge didn't belittle the importance of what Raine had told her. A kiss might be a small thing in another relationship, but between Raine and Gabe…

"Well, you are friends," she said carefully.

"It wasn't that kind of a kiss." Raine closed her eyes. She didn't know why she was telling her mother this.

"On occasion, I have wondered," her mother confessed softly.

Raine's eyes opened. "You what?"

"Well, he has always watched over you. Done things for you, taken you places…all the time you were growing up."

"Mom!" Raine was suddenly indignant. "The way you make it sound—"

Marge wasn't deterred. "I saw his face one time when you came back for a visit, then had to leave again the next day. He came with us to the airport, remember? And when you walked away he looked so…" She shrugged, unable to find the proper word.

"No, Mom."

"He was always asking after you."

"*Mom!* Stop it! I'm not going to listen to this!" Raine jumped up from the chair.

Marge folded her hands in her lap, frowning.

"That would explain so much," she murmured, uttering her thoughts aloud.

"Mom, I'm leaving. I'm going back to Gabe's house."

"But that doesn't explain *your* reaction, does it?" She looked up at her daughter, her brown eyes soft with love and curiosity.

Raine caught her breath. Unerringly, her mother had cut straight through to the crux of the matter. It wasn't Gabe who had the problem, it was Raine herself! But she didn't believe for one second what her mom had intimated about Gabe. It was an idea that had just occurred to her, and she was speculating about it out loud. She did that a lot.

But there was no denying what Raine had told her: that she had wanted to kiss Gabe back. "It's—it's what you said the other day," Raine said desperately. "Serendipity. Or—or gratitude! Look what he's doing for me! I'm not in my normal state of mind. My hormones are raging! I fall asleep at ten p.m.! I cry at the drop of a hat!" She paced across the room, then spun back around. "I don't know why I bothered to come over here," she cried dramatically. "I could have stayed at home and been just as miserable!"

"Why are you miserable, Raine?" her mother asked, again cutting to the core of the matter.

Raine lifted her hands in frustration and hurried out of the house.

SHE COULDN'T settle down at all that afternoon. She wanted to go out somewhere, but she didn't know where. She also didn't want to be alone, yet didn't want to be with anyone.

She ended up taking a nap, only to be awakened by a knock on the kitchen door. It wasn't the family knock.

Frowning, she straightened her blouse and slacks and ran a hand over her hair. Who could it be? Gabe hadn't warned her to expect anyone.

She opened the door without checking, her New York caution having been tempered by the far less dangerous atmosphere of Tyler, and found her mother standing on the doorstep. Her face was drained of color, her eyes huge with a recent shock.

"Mom?" Raine questioned, alarmed.

"Raine?" Her mother's throat seemed to be extremely dry. "There's someone..." She swallowed. "There's someone at my house. He says—he says his name is Joel Hastings!"

CHAPTER THIRTEEN

A HOST OF THOUGHTS raced through Raine's mind. But the dominant one was *Joel...here?* She stared blankly at her mother.

"Raine...*Raine!*" Her mother tugged on her sleeve. "He's the baby's father, isn't he? Isn't that the name you told me?"

Raine nodded, still unable to speak.

Marge ran a hand through her hair, mussing it but not caring. "Oh, God, Raine. What should I do? Do you want me to send him over here? Or—or maybe it would be better if you came to our place. I didn't tell him where you were, just that I'd get you."

"I—I'll come," she said.

"Thank goodness Gabe is at work today," Marge said as she tugged on Raine's sleeve again, this time to get her to move. "I don't even want to think about what would happen if he... And George is still off playing golf. He should be gone for at least another hour. He usually has dinner with his cronies afterward."

They moved across the yard, through the hedge, then across the other yard. Raine functioned as if she were in a daze. She let her mother guide her into the other house and through it to the cozy living room.

A man stood up. Joel! Dark and sleek and masculinely beautiful. He was dressed in a casual silk suit that Raine knew cost almost as much as her mother and George had paid for the renovation of their house. From a center part, his hair fell in loose black curls to his shoulders. When he moved, it was with pantherlike grace.

"Lorraine…" he said, his dark gaze fixed only on her.

"Joel," Raine returned tautly. She didn't rush over to him as he seemed to expect.

His gaze was intense, then it broke away to include Marge. "Your mother has been so kind to let me wait here for you. But Lorraine, if we might talk in private?"

If anything, Marge's stance became more obstinate. She planted her feet firmly in the carpet and crossed her arms. She wasn't about to budge, not unless it came at her daughter's request. Raine's heart swelled with love for her.

"It's all right, Mom," she said. "It might be best if we talked on our own."

Marge's arms slowly unfolded. "You're sure?" she asked.

"I'm positive."

"Well," Marge said, "I'm just going to be in the next room. You call out if you need anything." And for good measure she gave Joel a hard look before she left.

Joel was amused at her mother's protectiveness. A smile tugged at his lips. "Your mother is a tiger when it comes to someone she loves. I see where you get it."

"I'm not a tiger, Joel," Raine denied.

"I seem to remember a few times when I called you that."

"Joel!" she exclaimed sharply. She didn't need any oblique references to their past lovemaking. "Let's get directly to the point. What do you want?"

His eyes widened. "Why you, of course."

Raine's knees wobbled. He still had the power to unsettle her.

He continued, "You must admit that your news came as a surprise. That's why I—"

"I told you I was going to a doctor," she interrupted, "and I told you why…what I was going to check for."

"Still, it was a shock. It wasn't something we planned."

"I didn't plan it either, Joel," she said.

"Have you done as I suggested?" he asked quietly.

"No."

His eyes narrowed. "So you're determined to have this baby?"

"Yes."

He continued to look at her. "Then I'll marry you," he said.

Raine couldn't believe what she'd heard. This wasn't the Joel she knew, the man she was intimately familiar with. Her Joel wasn't at all shy about expressing his disregard for the institution of marriage. Freedom was a living thing to him, as necessary to his everyday life as his devotion to the dance.

"Lorraine," he said somewhat impatiently. "Did you hear what I said? I want to marry you!"

"Why?" Raine asked.

"Because when you left…I missed you."

"You mean, you *want* to be a father?"

"If that gets you back, yes!"

Raine shook her head. First he wanted her, then when she got pregnant, he wanted her but not the baby, now he was willing to take them both? "It's too late for that, Joel."

"It's never too late!" he exclaimed. "I love you! I've never loved anyone the way I love you. I want you to come back. And if it's what you want, we'll transform our little nest—fill it with baby things. Tricycles, bicycles…bats and balls. The park is just across the street. I'm quite good at baseball, did you know that?"

"I'm married, Joel," she said quietly.

"And football. I detest it, but I can teach—" He broke off. "What did you say?"

Raine repeated softly, "I said I'm married."

"You're kidding!"

She showed him her ring.

Joel paled. "But it's my baby," he said.

"Yes, it is. But the last time we talked, you didn't want it. You told me to get rid of it. To sweep it out of the way. Out of sight, out of mind! So I left."

"Lorraine—" he caught hold of her arm "—this has to be some kind of mistake. I want you! I love you! I was…stunned, that's all. I wasn't thinking right. I didn't mean…"

"It's far too late."

"Who?" he demanded angrily. "Tell me who this husband of yours is. I'll have a talk with him and—"

She pulled her arm away.

"No!" he cried. "I won't accept this!" For the first time since she'd met him Joel wasn't the master of his universe.

Marge shot back into the room, fire in her eyes at

the sound of his raised voice. "Do you need help, Raine?" she demanded.

Joel turned on her. "Are you behind this?" he demanded. "Did you arrange for Lorraine to marry...whoever the country bumpkin is? Do you realize the damage you're doing?"

"Don't talk to my mother like that, Joel," Raine warned him.

He swept a thick curl of hair away from his face. "I'm going to get you back, Lorraine," he promised.

"And I'm going to show you to the door." Marge lifted her arm and pointed the way.

"Lorraine!" Joel protested.

Raine turned her back.

He came up close behind her, but didn't touch her. "All right," he said tightly. "You seem determined to make this difficult. And, yes, maybe I deserve it. But I'm not going to go away. Not until you agree to come back with me. I'm staying at a place not far from here. Timber something-or-other. It's an Addison hotel, thank God. At least your little backwater can do something right!"

"Goodbye and good riddance," Marge murmured as she closed the front door behind him.

Raine sank to the couch and covered her face with her hands. She didn't know what she thought about anything at the moment. She had never expected Joel to come here, to say what he had. Once she had hoped, but now...

Her mother stroked her bright hair. "He's handsome in a flashy kind of way, but his manners could certainly use some polishing. What did you see in him, Raine? No, never mind. People don't always stop to analyze things before they fall in love."

Raine lowered her hands. "There's more to him than what you saw. He can be sweet and funny. He can!" she insisted at her mother's doubtful look.

"What is he?" Marge asked. "An actor?"

"He's a dancer…a choreographer. He designs all the dancers' movements on stage."

"Is that how you met him?"

Raine nodded. "He's very well-known."

"He thinks a lot of himself."

"So do other people."

"Still…" Marge watched her carefully. "What are you going to do?"

Raine looked away. "I don't know. What if what he said is true? What if, deep down, he was afraid, confused…and now he's not? He can be selfish and vain, but he can also be very vulnerable. I wouldn't have cared for him otherwise. Do I have the right to keep him and his child apart?"

"What about Gabe?"

She groaned. "Mom…I don't know."

"What about the way you feel about *him?*"

"It was purely a figment of my imagination."

"That's not what you thought earlier."

Raine groaned again.

Marge straightened. "Well, at least you're going to have some time to think about it. Gabe won't be home until tomorrow morning."

THE KEY TURNED in the front-door lock. Next, the door swung open, then shut. Gabe was being careful to mute every sound. But Raine was already awake and waiting for him on the couch, curled against an arm, a crocheted throw spread over her legs.

Not seeing her, he moved across the dimly lit room

and was about to enter the hall when finally she stirred. "Gabe?" she said softly, not wanting to startle him.

He wheeled around, automatically narrowing his gaze. "Raine?" he questioned.

She stood up, draping the throw over the back of the couch. She was fully dressed. In fact, she hadn't changed for bed last night because she hadn't thought to go there. Not even her recent urge to go to sleep early had overtaken her.

"Gabe, we need to talk," she said levelly.

He stood so still he might have been a statue. "What about?" he asked.

"Have you had breakfast?" she said, closing in on him.

"At the station. Raine, what is it? You look—"

"Come with me," she said, and brought him to sit beside her on the couch.

"I'm not sure I like the looks of this," he murmured gruffly.

Raine took a breath and said, "I have something to tell you. Joel is in Tyler."

At first he seemed unable to place the name, then recognition dawned. "*The* Joel?" he demanded.

"He came to Mom's yesterday evening."

"How did he know where to find you?"

"I didn't exactly keep the fact that I'm from Tyler a secret. People knew. So did he."

Gabe sat forward. "What does he want?"

Raine hesitated before answering honestly, "Me."

"Well, he can't have you."

"Gabe—"

"Don't 'Gabe' me! After the way he's treated you? Does he think he can just waltz right in and whisk you away? Take you back to New York so he can start treating you badly all over again? You should have more sense than that, Raine. What are you? A glutton for punishment?''

''I didn't say that I—''

He ran a hand over the back of his neck, his expression tight. ''I really thought you had more sense, Raine. What does your mother say?''

''My *mother* thinks I have enough sense to make up my mind myself!''

''I want to talk to him. I want to tell him exactly what I...''

Gabe heard himself rant on and on, a wild reaction to a mortal pain. He was going to lose her! No matter what he did, no matter what he said, she was going to go away. With that *Joel* from New York.

It had been Gabe's greatest fear all along.

''No!'' she said. ''I don't want you to do that, Gabe. It wouldn't be productive.''

''I don't want to be *productive*. I want to knock his block off!''

''Gabe!'' She tried to calm him. ''This isn't like you.''

''How do you know?'' he challenged. ''How do you know I don't knock somebody's block off every chance I get? Twice a week, if I feel like it!''

She giggled unsteadily, and he relented. Raine's well-being was his prime concern. What he felt didn't matter. When he looked at her closely, he could see the signs of her distress.

He forced himself to take several long, deep breaths. ''All right,'' he said after a moment. ''Let's start over. You say he's here. Where?''

''At Timberlake Lodge.''

"How long is he going to stay?"

"He says until I agree to go back with him."

"And how long will it take before you do that?"

"Gabe, I never said—"

"All right, all right." He sighed again. He'd thought he'd had to face some hard things before in his life, but they were nothing compared to this!

"Did you stay up all night?" he asked, eyeing her creased clothing.

"I couldn't sleep."

"Then let's both hit the sack for a couple of hours. I didn't get much sleep last night either. There was a nasty fire in some old warehouses out by the highway. It took forever to put out." He stood up slowly, his body stiff and sore. "Then we'll talk. Okay?"

"Okay," she said softly.

Raine followed him into the hall, but within seconds she had ducked under his arm, wrapping her arm around his waist. He stiffened, but in the end he accepted her offer of support. Because it might be the last time they would be so close?

At the door to their separate rooms they parted. Over the past few days everything between them had been so derailed. The avoidances, the palpable tension whenever they were near each other.

"Gabe, I—" she started to say.

He reached out to stop her, his fingers gently touching her lips. "We'll talk about it later," he said huskily.

Her eyes, bright with tears, fell away from his.

Gabe struggled within himself, with the temptation to go for all or nothing. It would be so easy at this moment to toss caution to the wind, to loosen the bonds that had previously prevented him from taking what he wanted.

But his love for her was too great. He didn't want to make things worse than they already were. He didn't want her to hate him.

His hand slowly returned to his side and he forced an easygoing smile. "See you in a little while, Red," he said. Then he flicked the tip of her nose with his finger and disappeared into his room.

RAINE STILL couldn't sleep. Her mind was too busy, her heart too full. She'd gotten exactly what she'd wanted a short few weeks ago. Joel had come after her, ready to accept the baby, demanding that she return to him. But now that she had it, she wasn't so sure it was what she truly wanted. Was she that fickle? That shallow? Or had something much more portentous happened in the meantime?

She felt as if she were trembling on the brink of discovery. As if she were standing in front of a closed curtain beyond which might be either a spectacular new world…or chaos.

And instead of Joel, her concern was for Gabe. What he thought. What he felt. What he wanted.

Why? Why should it matter?

Love? The word muscled its way back into her consciousness. And once again she fled from it, afraid to admit that it could be true.

GABE STOOD in front of the open window in his bedroom. In the distance storm clouds were building. It seemed an apt reflection of his life.

Joel wanted Raine to come back to him. He was the baby's father. Raine had been shattered when he'd rejected her. Didn't it stand to reason that after a short period of making him squirm she would welcome the penitent back?

Where did all of this leave him? Gabe wondered. His only claim to her was a scrap of paper—the wedding certificate that Sarah Kenton had given them upon their marriage.

A paper marriage. With no ties that bind.

But did Joel love her? Really love her...as *he* did? Gabe had to be sure.

A ROLLING CLAP of thunder awakened Raine. Her body jerked to instant alertness. The room was darker now than when she'd gone to sleep. Wind rattled the windowpanes. Suddenly, rain peppered down, sure to soak anything or anyone caught outside in it.

Raine jumped up and hurried to the windows, to be certain none was open to the storm. She checked every one except those in Gabe's room.

Surely that loud clap of thunder had awakened him as well. But when she put her ear to the door, she heard no sounds of movement from within.

"Gabe?" she called and tapped lightly on the door.

When there was no answer she turned the knob and peeked inside.

"Gabe?" she said again. But the rumpled bed was empty, as was the room.

Instinctively, Raine knew where he was: at Timberlake Lodge. She clapped a hand over her mouth. Gabe had gone to confront Joel. To knock his block off, as he'd threatened earlier?

She jumped into action. Grabbing the poncho from the hook by the front door, she raced back through the house to the kitchen door. She checked the garage, but as she expected, it was empty as well. He had taken the Explorer.

Immediately she switched to her second plan and darted across the yards in the teeming rain. She ignored the wet tendrils of hair that fell into her eyes and the drops of rain that dribbled down her neck.

Once again desperately in need during a storm, she rapped her knuckles against the hard wood of her mother's back door. "Mom! It's me. Raine!"

But where before there'd been no answer, this time footsteps hurried through the house and soon the door swung open.

"Raine?" her mother said, taken slightly aback.

Raine didn't have time for formalities. "Mom! Gabe's gone to the lodge! Can I borrow your car?"

Marge blinked at the unexpected request. She noted her daughter's agitated state, then looked at the teeming rain. "No. With the state you're in, I'd better drive."

Raine hugged her mother's neck, inadvertently getting her wet. "Oh, thank you, Mom. Thank you! I'm afraid there might be a fight."

Marge collected her purse from the counter, called something to George, then bustled out of the house, shaking open an umbrella, which she held over their heads all the way to the detached garage. "Are you thinking that Gabe... No, Raine, not Gabe!"

"He's angry at Joel for what he did to me."

"So am I, but I'm not going to beat him up."

Marge opened the garage's side door and they both piled into the Lincoln. The main door opened at the touch of a remote-control button. Within seconds they were backing out.

"I don't know what else to do, Mom. I told Gabe and he said he needed some sleep, then we'd talk... and when I woke up, he was gone."

"That doesn't sound like Gabe, either. He keeps his word."

"I know! Everything's so... *Nothing* is normal now!"

From that point on Marge had to give her full attention to the road, and Raine stayed quiet so that she could concentrate.

CHAPTER FOURTEEN

THE STORM HAD LET UP by the time Raine and her mother drove into the lodge's parking lot. The strong wind gusts had ceased and the rain had slackened to a drizzle. They had no trouble spotting the Explorer. Marge parked next to it, and she and Raine hopped out.

"Do you know Joel's room number?" Marge asked.

"He didn't say."

Marge looked at her watch. "It's only nine o'clock. He could be eating breakfast."

"Do you think...? No, Gabe wouldn't create a scene in the restaurant."

"An angry man doesn't always care where he is when he picks a fight."

They hurried in through the main doors. Marge went to the front desk, while Raine jogged on to the restaurant. All the tables were orderly and quiet, the dozen or so people eating at them the ultimate in decorum.

She met her mother back in the lobby. "Not there," she reported.

"They're not in his room, either. I tried calling on the house phone."

"But where..."

Something caught Marge's eye just over Raine's

shoulder. She frowned, squinted, then allowed a tiny satisfied smile. "Look," she directed her daughter.

Raine turned around. Across the lobby, in a somewhat isolated conversation area, Gabe and Joel sat talking. Neither man looked scuffed or bruised. Neither seemed to be angry.

Raine released a long breath. She looked back at her mother and, somewhat chagrined, murmured, "A false alarm."

"Maybe we'd better get over there," Marge suggested, "before something goes wrong."

The two men didn't notice them until they were practically upon them. Gabe was first on his feet, but Joel was the first to speak.

"Lorraine!" he said, smiling as he reached out to her. His kiss skimmed her cheek when she turned her head. "And Mother, too."

"Mr. Hastings," Marge replied tersely.

Joel's dark eyes were proprietary as he looked at Raine. Then he turned to Gabe and said boastfully, "*This* is my Lorraine. The wonderful girl I was telling you about. Can you imagine her happily married to a country bumpkin and actually wanting to live in a place like this?" Joel laughed. "You can see just by looking at her that she doesn't belong here."

Raine stared at Gabe. He hadn't yet told Joel who he was.

"I don't remember catching your name..." Joel continued, frowning slightly. Then, not waiting for a reply, he turned back to Raine. "Have you changed your mind? Are you ready to come back with me?"

"What do you think you're doing, Gabe?" Raine asked, her gaze fixed on him. She wasn't sure what she felt at that moment. She'd been so worried, and was now so stunned to find him here, acting as if nothing untoward had occurred.

"I'm not doing anything, except having a little friendly talk with Joel, here."

Joel's frown deepened. "Gabe?" he repeated.

"The country bumpkin," Raine explained shortly.

"The husband?" Joel inferred, startled.

"One and the same," Gabe returned smoothly.

"But you never—never said…" Joel stammered.

"I didn't need to. You did most of the talking."

Joel collected himself. He shook his mane of beautiful hair. "That was not a gentlemanly thing to do."

"Neither is rejecting the woman you made pregnant."

"Gabe," Raine said warningly.

The two men glared at each other. Then Joel turned again to Raine and said, "Now I can see that it's even more important for you to come back to New York. The man's a bully, Raine. Do you think he'll let you resume your career?"

"He's worth *ten* of you!" Marge chimed in, coming to Gabe's defense.

"He's a Neanderthal," Joel decreed.

"You're good at calling people names," Gabe said, his hands curling into tighter fists.

Raine thrust herself between them, aware of the people in the lobby who'd paused to watch. "That's enough!" she said with suppressed vehemence. "*I'm* the one who decides what I will and will not do. And I will not stand here and watch as the two of you act like twelve-year-old boys! Joel, you're being rude. Gabe…you have no business being here."

"I had to see things for myself, Raine," Gabe said, "before—"

Raine cut him off. "I don't want to hear any more."

Joel smirked. "Yes, go away, hayseed."

Gabe lunged forward. Raine stopped him by placing a hand on his chest. His heart beat strongly beneath her fingers.

Raine had a hard time meeting his smoldering gaze. "Please, Gabe? Go home," she pleaded. "I'm going to stay and talk with Joel. After that, you and I will talk...like we were going to do earlier." She looked at her mother. "Could I borrow the car again, Mom, and you go back with Gabe?"

"I'll take you back," Joel volunteered.

Raine shook her head. "No, I want to do this on my own."

Marge murmured worriedly, "Are you sure? I can stay...."

"Completely on my own," Raine replied.

Marge nodded. "Come on, Gabe. Let's do as Raine asks."

Gabe gave Raine another long look, then he let himself be pulled away after Marge passed her daughter her car keys.

Once they were alone, Joel reached out to bring her close. "Come on," he said. "Let's go to my room."

Raine pulled away. "No, we'll talk here."

Joel glanced around the lobby. It was growing thicker with people. "But there's no privacy here."

"Exactly."

He smiled. "Is it because you're afraid to be alone with me?"

Raine chose the chair Gabe had used earlier. "Not at all," she said.

Joel perched uncomfortably opposite her.

Raine watched him, wondering how she could have ever thought herself in love with him. She was lucky to have this moment. To be able to come to this realization. It would set her free.

Maybe she was stronger than she had once thought. Not as strong as her mother, but growing stronger. When she'd found herself pregnant and alone, it seemed as if her world had shattered. Emotionally, she'd reverted to childhood and come running home.

Now, seeing Joel out of his element, observing how negatively he had reacted to people she cared for, what he thought of her hometown, she realized that it was the world she had created with him that had been false. It had had all the constancy of a soap bubble. No wonder it had shattered. Except for the child...

Raine was surprised by the sudden warmth that flooded over her when she thought of the child. Of the little girl or boy...growing up in Tyler.

"I'm not going back with you, Joel," she said calmly, levelly. "You'll have to accept that. Just like I'll have to accept the fact that I'm limited in my talent as a dancer. I've been in a few good shows here and there, but I was never the star. I never will be. Only a select few ever can. Once, I wanted that more than anything. Now—" she shrugged "—it doesn't seem important. Maybe it's the baby. Maybe because of it, I'm finally growing up."

"You're a very good dancer, Lorraine!" Joel said.

"I'm good, not great. Be honest with me, Joel. Please."

His eyes dropped away and she had her answer. It hurt, but in another way, it was a relief.

"Now," she said, "be equally honest. Do you really want this child?"

"Of course I do!" he exclaimed, his handsome features strained. "I want you!"

"But it would be better if there wasn't a child," she stated.

His eyes slid away again.

"I thought so," Raine said softly. "And, Joel, that's all right. I'm not trying to judge you or make you feel bad. You were very up-front with me from the beginning about not wanting children. Some people don't. But it would be a mistake for me to come back to you if that's truly the way you feel. It wouldn't be fair to the child or to you. I *want* this baby. I wasn't sure at first, but I am now. And when I have it, I don't expect anything from you. Not money, not active parenting. The baby will know who you are, though, and what you do. And if you ever change your mind and want to come into its life, you can. I won't stand in the way."

"But I love you!" he declared.

Raine smiled, able to think of him again with some fondness since he no longer had the power to hurt her. "In your own fashion, I believe you do. For you to come here, to offer marriage..." She touched the back of her fingers to his cheek.

The magnitude of what he'd lost and might never have opportunity to possess again was reflected momentarily in his eyes, but the introspection didn't last. It wasn't in his nature to be reflective. "What will you do?" he asked. "Stay with the bumpkin?"

"His name is Gabe Atwood and he's a very good

friend." Then, in answer to his question, she said simply, "I don't know."

Joel caught her hand and kissed her fingers. "Will you let me know when the baby's born? At the very least I'd like to know if I have a son or a daughter."

"Of course," Raine promised in all good faith.

THE SUN WAS OUT and birds were chirping contentedly when Raine pulled into the driveway at her mother's house. It was hard to realize that there had been a recent storm in the area, except for the puddles and the occasional drop of water that fell from a leaf.

Raine put the car away in the garage, then tapped on her mother's back door.

"Is everything all right?" Marge asked cautiously.

"Better than it has been in a long time," Raine replied, handing over the set of keys.

"And Joel?" Marge ventured.

"Is on his way back to New York."

Relief washed the tension from her mother's face. All she said, though, was "Good."

Raine started toward Gabe's house.

"Raine," her mother called, "he's not there. He dropped me off and said he was going for a ride."

Raine pulled up. "Did he say where?"

"No, but Raine…he was upset. I could tell."

Raine continued to the house and let herself inside.

GABE PARKED the Explorer and got out to walk across the rolling hills that skirted Timber Lake. He retraced the path he and Raine had taken the day they'd come here, during a time when he'd harbored some hope for their future together.

He was careful not to look toward the lodge, even if he could have seen it through the thick branches of the trees. Some would say he was masochistic even for coming this close. But he couldn't stop himself.

He hadn't liked Joel Hastings. But had he expected to? The man's way of thinking and behaving—particularly his shameful treatment of Raine—was in diametric opposition to his own. The man's selfishness, his grandiose ego might be tolerated in the world of the theater, but not in Tyler. And this was Tyler.

Gabe's murmured curse frightened a squirrel. The furry creature scurried up a tree and sat on a branch, flicking its tail and fussing at him. Gabe might have found the occasion funny if it hadn't been for the fact that his life was coming apart.

Raine now had two reasons to go back to New York—the baby's father and the stage. And there was absolutely nothing Gabe could do about it. Richard had said to tell her the truth, but he couldn't! The fact that he loved her paled in comparison to the life that awaited her in New York, if only she said the word.

Gabe tramped on, torturing himself with the knowledge that at that very moment Raine could be in Joel's room at the lodge, making up with him and giving her assent.

RAINE WAITED for Gabe to return home. She tried to stay awake, but with no sleep last night and barely an hour this morning, she found her effort doomed.

Little by little she got more and more comfortable on the couch, and before she knew it, she was stretched out fully on the cushions.

She had no idea what time the sirens awakened her. They seemed to fill her head, coming at her from all sides. But as she shook off the latent grogginess, she realized that they were converging a distance away.

She struggled to her feet and went into the kitchen to make a cup of tea. Then she realized that she was hungry. She'd had nothing to eat all day. As she toasted a piece of bread and spread peanut butter on it, she wondered about Gabe. Where was he? What was he doing? Had he eaten? Was he still upset?

Raine wished he'd come home. She wanted to talk to him, to tell him what she'd done about Joel and how she felt as a result. Tell him of the newfound strength she'd discovered inside herself. Tell him…what? That she loved him?

Raine still shied away from the word. It seemed so odd to think like that in connection with Gabe, to think in anything more than a sisterly way. But she had been freed this afternoon. She could see so many things clearly now. The way in which, in the past, she'd thought herself to be in love, yet always found something lacking in the men she chose. Had she unconsciously been comparing them to Gabe? Looking to them for his kindness, for his strength of character, for his genuineness?

Had she been blinded by the years they'd spent together as friends? Kept up the old way of seeing him in order not to have to face the truth?

She wanted him to come home, so they could talk about it. So she could tell him…

Raine stopped herself. She was acting too much like Joel! Concentrating on what *she* thought, on how *she* felt, on what *she* wanted. But what about Gabe?

Didn't he get a choice? Would it be fair for her to reveal her newfound feelings for him when she knew that, in all likelihood, it would cement him to this marriage...whether or not it was what he truly wanted?

When they'd first entered into this arrangement it had had a finite life. One day the marriage would end—probably not so long after the baby was born. How could she, on her own, alter that?

Gabe deserved better. He deserved to marry someone he loved, someone who wasn't carrying another man's child. She couldn't allow him to continue this farce from a heightened sense of obligation. She had to free him as well.

Loving someone was knowing when to let go. Where had she heard that before?

The familiar series of taps sounded on the kitchen door, and when Raine went to answer it she found her mother and George standing outside. Both were unusually pale.

Raine frowned. "What is it?"

Marge came inside and made her sit down.

"What is it?" Raine whispered, a cold hand closing around her heart.

Her mother answered quietly, tersely. "We've just had some news...from Joe. Raine, there's been a fire at Mrs. Franklin's house. You remember Mrs. Franklin? Your teacher in second grade?"

Raine nodded. "I remember her. Mom, what *is* it?" Her voice had gone all wavery from fear.

"Gabe must have been driving by her house when he saw the smoke. He put in a call, then ran inside. I'm sure it was to find Mrs. Franklin..."

Her mother continued to talk, but Raine was no longer able to follow. Her brain had started to spin.

"...All right...alive." She caught individual snatches of her mother's words.

"Gabe...or Mrs. Franklin?" Raine interrupted at last. "Who's alive? *Who?*"

"Why, *both* of them, dear," Marge replied. "Mrs. Franklin wasn't at home. She was down the street at a neighbor's house. But it might have been better for Gabe if she had been home, because he wouldn't stop looking for her. No, wait!" She intervened when Raine started to get up. "Like I said, Gabe is alive, but he's been taken to the hospital."

Raine's gaze jerked to George. "How bad is he?" she breathed.

Marge answered for her husband. "Joe couldn't tell. He was at Granny Rose's and ran down the street when he saw the smoke and heard the fire engines stop. He saw some fire fighters administer oxygen to Gabe, then they put him in an ambulance."

"Was he burned?" Raine asked tightly.

"We don't know," Marge said. She rubbed Raine's arm, trying to give solace. "What do you want to do, dear? If you want to go to the hospital, George and I will take you. If you want to stay here, George will go alone, I'll stay here and he'll call as soon as he learns anything."

"I'm going," Raine said, standing up.

CHAPTER FIFTEEN

HOSPITALS ALWAYS MADE Raine highly uncomfortable—the smells, the unfamiliar images, the doctors and nurses with godlike power.

George, however, was in his element as they stepped through the doors of the emergency department. He consulted with the head nurse before sweeping them through the halls and onto an elevator to an upper floor. "He's been moved," he said tersely.

The doors popped open and they stepped out. George led them to the nursing station of the intensive care unit. "Gabriel Atwood?" he demanded.

"Yes, Doctor." The nurse on duty checked a file. "This way."

Raine didn't let her gaze stray from the pattern of floor tiles that were eaten up as they walked. Three whites, a tan, and three whites again. She knew when they moved into a room filled with equipment and stopped at the side of a bed. But she was afraid to look up. Afraid to see how badly Gabe was hurt. Tears glistened in her eyes as she gathered her strength and slowly lifted them...and met Gabe's clear blue gaze.

"Hi, Red," he rasped, grinning.

Raine stepped closer. "Gabe?" she whispered.

"Just a little singed," he teased, then he started to

cough—hard, racking coughs that he found difficult to control. "Sorry," he apologized when it was over.

"We were so worried, Gabe," Marge murmured.

Raine examined him as her mother spoke. His face and hands were reddened, as were his neck and ears. Black soot still clung stubbornly to his skin in places in spite of the nursing staff's best efforts.

"I'm all right," he said. "I've been…worse." He started to cough again.

A nurse asked them to step outside, and Raine led the way into the hall. As soon as they were out of Gabe's hearing, she turned on George. "Has he?" she demanded crisply. "Has he been worse than this? Why is he in intensive care if it's not—"

George spoke calmly. "He's in intensive care because the doctor wants to keep a close eye on him. It's obvious he's breathed in a lot of hot, smoky gases. He also has some burns. They don't look bad right now, but the doctor will want to wait and see. Sometimes the true nature of a burn doesn't show up until the next day. The breathing passage to his lungs is also irritated. It can swell and cause problems. If it does, or if the burns need more attention, it's far better for him to be here." He paused. "Then again, everything could be exactly as it looks at first glance and he could be released tomorrow."

"Tomorrow?" Raine echoed hopefully.

"*If* everything is satisfactory. Gabe's a strong young man in top condition, and he doesn't smoke…which helps a lot."

"You can go back in now," the nurse said from behind them.

"You go, Raine," Marge urged her. "George and

I will wait out here. You and Gabe…well, you need to be alone."

Raine walked slowly back to the specialized-care room. This time she saw all the machines. Gabe was hooked up to a couple of them.

A cough racked his body. "Ow," he complained when he was done, rubbing his chest. He gave her a deprecating little smile.

"I wish I could do something to help," she murmured.

"Occupational hazard," he said. "Happens all the time. Sometimes even when we're wearing…our equipment. All it takes is one…wrong breath."

"You weren't wearing *any* equipment."

"Well, no."

"Why did you do it, Gabe? Why didn't you wait for the others to arrive?"

"Mrs. Franklin."

"I don't know how to tell you—"

"I've heard. She was down the street."

"So all this—" she indicated his injuries "—was for nothing."

He caught hold of her hand and changed the subject. "He doesn't love you enough, Raine."

Raine didn't trust herself enough in that moment to discuss the situation. Not with him lying there looking so vulnerable. Not with the fear she'd carried with her to the hospital still ricocheting in her mind. She might say something she'd later regret.

"Gabe, this isn't the right time. Your lungs… You shouldn't talk."

"Just promise me you won't leave before I get home. Before I…" He started to cough again—deep, hard coughs that this time didn't cease.

Raine looked around frantically for a nurse. Gabe needed help and she didn't know what to do! She went to the door and met a nurse already hurrying to the room.

"You're going to have to leave now," the woman said as she made her way to the head of the bed.

"Gabe..." Raine called earnestly. It was a plea for him not to get sicker.

"Now!" the nurse directed, not looking back. Her attention was fully with her patient.

Tears flooded Raine's eyes. She was so worried for him! She made her way down the hall and into her mother's arms.

"Oh, Mom," she cried, and Marge cradled her gently to her breast.

RAINE WOULDN'T LEAVE the hospital until exhaustion forced her to. "Think of the child," George had admonished her in his best professional tone. "I've spoken to Gabe's doctor, I've spoken to the head ICU nurse. If there's even the slightest change for the worse in his condition, someone will call and we'll be here in five minutes. You can't do anything to help him by stressing yourself or the baby."

Raine was an emotional wreck as they drove home. The silent tears she shed were even more telling than if she had wailed and moaned.

Her mother wouldn't hear of her spending the night alone. She made up the bed in the spare room and Raine curled into it, too tired to do anything more than sniff as her head rested on the pillow.

Raine slept past noon the next day and no one disturbed her. Her first thought upon awakening was of Gabe. As she hurried into the kitchen, her mother glanced up from reading the newspaper.

"Have you heard anything?" Raine asked breathlessly.

"He's doing fine, at last report. The burns aren't serious, and he didn't have any more trouble with his breathing last night. George stopped off to see him when he visited one of his patients. He said Gabe was still coughing up soot, but that's to be expected for a day or two."

"Coughing up soot?" Raine repeated.

"From all the smoke he breathed. His lungs are clearing themselves, George says. That's what they're supposed to do."

"So he's not..."

"In any danger? No. You can relax on that score. He's past the worst."

Raine collapsed into one of the barrel-shaped chairs that clustered around her mother's kitchen table and let her head fall onto her folded arms. "Thank God," she murmured huskily. "I was so afraid."

She sensed her mother's intense scrutiny, but when Marge spoke, it wasn't about her and Gabe.

"Gabe's quick action probably saved Mrs. Franklin's house. Chief Sorenson said that with all those newspapers and magazines stacked on her back porch and all those school papers stored in her attic, it was a wonder the place didn't go up like a tinderbox. Do you know she kept drawings and writing exercises of all of her students from more than forty years of teaching? Chief Sorenson said he doesn't think she ever threw anything away. He said if the fire had reached the attic before it was noticed, they'd probably still be trying to put out the blaze. As it is, the kitchen's going to have to be rebuilt—that's where the fire started. She put something on to cook and forgot it. Just walked out of the house to go visiting. And the back porch—it's pretty well gone now, as well as the room above.''

''What's going to happen to her?'' Raine asked, lifting her head.

''Well, you know her grandson wants her to go live at Worthington House…and so does his sister. But I understand there's a niece who's been widowed for several years, and who's offered to move in with her, but her offer's never been accepted. Maybe now it will be. A ninety-two-year-old woman can be only so independent. Especially when she's getting forgetful.''

''Her whole life is in that house,'' Raine said. ''All her furniture and keepsakes.''

''It's all safe, but pretty smoky right now. Half the town's volunteered to help clean up.'' Marge paused. ''What's upset her most is that Gabe got hurt looking for her.''

''Gabe wouldn't want that.''

''No.''

''Maybe—maybe I should go talk with her,'' Raine murmured.

''That might be a good idea. It would also give you something to do, to stop you worrying.''

''You just told me I had nothing to worry about!''

Her mother smiled. ''I know, and you don't, but that's never stopped someone who loves a person from being worried until they can see him or her with their own eyes.''

Raine felt a shiver run down her back. "What makes you think that I—"

"I'm not blind, Raine. And you practically told me the other day, remember? You should have seen the way you looked last night. Why, if I'd had any doubt…"

Raine stood up. "I'm going back to Gabe's house," she announced, cutting her mother off before the fateful word could be uttered again. "Then—then I'm going to go see Mrs. Franklin."

"Richard brought the Explorer home last night. He thought you might have need of it."

Raine paused. "Richard?"

"He came to the hospital yesterday evening. So did other friends of Gabe's. You don't remember?"

"No."

"Joe, Britt, Nora…"

"No."

Raine's mother could only shake her head.

So SHE DIDN'T REMEMBER anyone coming to the hospital yesterday evening! So what?

Why not? her conscience challenged.

Because she'd been tired, she answered. Because of what she'd been through that day and for numerous days before.

Because she loved Gabe? her conscience insisted. *Because she loved him and was worried sick about his well-being? Because when she'd seen him, looking so gallant and so incapacitated in that hospital bed, her heart had twisted and squeezed to such an extent that it had become impossible for her to deny her true feelings for him any longer?*

Yes, yes…*yes!* she admitted. She loved him! She

loved him! Maybe she'd always loved him and just hadn't known it. Gabe had played such a large part in her life—been there when she needed him, been there when she didn't!

But how did he feel about her? There'd been that kiss…but could she deduce anything from it? He didn't want her to go back to Joel, but was that anything more than him acting as Gabe the protector?

Raine put the finishing touches on her makeup. She was going to go see Gabe before she saw Mrs. Franklin. He was the most important person in her life now, whether he knew it or not. No matter if he *ever* knew it.

She turned away from the bathroom mirror and gasped. Because Gabe stood in the doorway.

"Beautiful as ever," he murmured, his voice still raspy from the smoke.

The room suddenly didn't seem large enough. Nor did it contain enough air. She took a gulping breath and tried to remain steady.

"Gabe! I was just coming to see you."

He smiled slightly, that same sweet smile that now made her heart skip a beat.

"The doctor let me go early," he said. "I think the staff got tired of all the telephone calls."

"But are you…? Should you…? Just because they got tired…"

His smile deepened and he stepped back out of the doorway so she could pass, which she did, holding herself under rigid control.

"I'm fine," he said. "I didn't mean that literally. The doctor wouldn't have discharged me if he didn't—" he paused to cough, then looked sheepish "—didn't think I was ready to be let go."

"You don't sound fine."

"It's just a cough. Par for the course with smoke inhalation."

Raine led the way into the living room and to the couch, her thoughts scattered to the four winds. What had she planned to do? To say? How had she intended to handle this? She fell back on yesterday's decisions.

"Gabe, I—"

He allowed her to get no further. He took her hand and rested it on his thigh. Then he studied her fingers, as if suddenly they were of great interest. "Raine, yesterday I asked you to promise me something. I've been thinking about it. And I realize now that my request wasn't fair. Just because I don't think Joel loves you enough, it doesn't mean you feel the same way. I'm certainly no expert on love, that's for sure." He laughed lightly and coughed again.

"I've decided to make you another proposition," he continued determinedly. "If the baby is what's causing all the problems, if Joel still doesn't want it and you want to go back to him and to the stage...after the baby's born, you can leave it here with me. I'll give it my name and raise it as if it were my child. It won't make any difference to me that it's not. A child is a child. Children can't help how they come into the world." He paused to breathe carefully, as if what he'd said before had been a strain. "Your mother will be right next door. She'll help me. So will my dad. The baby won't want for attention."

Raine stared at him, stunned. Of all the things she might have thought Gabe would say, that wasn't one of them. "You'd raise my baby?" she breathed.

"To the best of my ability. The people in Tyler would accept it. I'd see to it that they did. There wouldn't be any problems for the child."

"You've thought this all through?"

"I didn't have much else to do after three o'clock yesterday afternoon."

"Except try to stay alive!" she retorted.

"I told you it wasn't that bad."

"I didn't believe you!"

He frowned, not comprehending her quick spurt of anger. "You don't like my proposition?"

Raine jerked her hand away and stood up. She couldn't stay still. She walked across the room and back. "I don't like the way you dismiss the dangerous conditions you work under. You might be used to them, but I'm not! I was afraid— I was afraid that you—" Twice her voice faltered, broke off. She couldn't put into words what had caused her such terror.

He frowned. "I did a stupid thing. But I thought Mrs. Franklin…"

Raine threw her hands up in frustration. "Are you trying to kill yourself in order to get away from me? Is that it? Well, Gabe, there are easier ways! If you want to end this marriage, it's simple. Tell me! We can have it annulled, get it dissolved. These past few weeks can be erased as if they never were. I don't care what people think anymore. I'm strong enough to handle it now. They can talk all they want, but I'll keep my head up. I don't have to have a husband. Not even you!"

Gabe sat forward. "I don't know what you're talking about. You're not making sense."

"This isn't a *real* marriage!"

"It was never meant to be."

"You don't want to be a father to another man's baby!"

"I just told you..." He stopped. The redness on his face and hands, caused by the fire, had grown no worse. But at that moment the ruddiness seemed to increase as blood drained from the uninjured portions of skin. "Is that what you want?" he demanded, his voice raspier than before. "Is this your way of telling me that you're ready to chuck it all in? He's come for you, so—"

"I'd never *chuck!*"

"That's what you're doing!"

"And what are you doing to me?" she returned. "You seem to assume that I'd choose my career over my baby! I'm the one who's going to carry it for nine months and then give birth, remember? If I hadn't wanted the baby, I wouldn't be doing this."

"So the answer is no."

"Yes...no...yes!" she shouted, slightly confused about which answer was correct. "I'm not going to leave the baby with you, because I'm not going to leave!"

Gabe became very still, his squall of anger depleted. He looked at her blankly. "You're not?"

"I sent Joel back to New York alone. I told him I wasn't going to come with him."

"But I thought—"

"You thought wrong."

Gabe ran a hand over his short hair and Raine saw that it was shaking. At that moment, as she was once again witness to his vulnerability, her anger was forgotten. She fell to her knees in front of him and gathered his hands into her own.

"Gabe," she pleaded, brushing his fingers with her lips. "I don't want to argue. Not about something unimportant. I was so worried about you. If anything had happened…"

Gabe moved like a man in a dream. He loosened a hand and cupped the back of her head. "What, Red?" he murmured. "What would have happened *if?*"

Raine looked at him. She couldn't hold back any longer. She had to tell him the truth. "I'd have died," she said simply.

Gabe's blue gaze moved over her, as if he were seeing her clearly for the first time.

"Why?" His question was almost a whisper.

Raine's heart thundered. "Because…I love you."

Gabe closed his eyes and, barely perceptibly, rocked back and forth. Then he moved forward until their foreheads rested against each other.

Raine's uneven breaths sounded loud to her ears. They seemed to fill the room. Then they were silenced as he tilted his head and captured her lips in a gentle, exploratory kiss that went on and on and on.…

A happiness Raine had never experienced before exploded within her, causing her to bubble over with laughter and tears when they finally broke apart.

Gabe, too, slid to the floor—his thighs against hers, his hips against hers. Then he started to kiss her again. Gently at first, then finally with open passion.

A wellspring of long-suppressed feeling suddenly opened up in Raine. She loved him! She loved him in a way she had never known existed before. Totally, completely, ultimately.

"Raine…" he murmured against her ear, his voice unsteady because of his depth of feeling. "Raine…" he continued to say her name over and over as he touched her. And he touched her as a man touches a woman he once thought forever out of his reach— reverently, deliriously, with avid hunger.

Could her mother have been correct? Could Gabe have loved her for a very long time—for years and years and years? Never saying anything because she was too blind to see? The thought made her love him all the more. Made her yield to whatever he wanted. To his questing lips and probing hands. She would have yielded completely, but he stopped.

"I want to do this right," he said.

Raine tried to pull them back to sanity. "You're hurt. You're just out of the hospital. Gabe…this can wait."

"Like hell it can," he growled. When he got up, he pulled her with him. Then he gathered her into his arms and lifted her, as if her weight was nothing…only to be overcome by another spell of coughing, which forced him to drop her back to her feet. "Not very romantic," he said.

Raine smiled. "I don't mind. I'm just glad you're safe. And up to now I hadn't expected rom—"

"Shh." He stopped her words with his lips. Moments later he murmured, "I can't…get enough. I'd hoped, but never expected—"

"It was me, Gabe. I didn't see."

He held her face between his hands and vowed, "I love you, Raine Peterson."

"And I love you," she returned softly, gazing into his wonderfully familiar face. "How—how long, Gabe?" she asked.

"Forever," he said.

Raine was unsure what he wanted to have happen next. What he had meant by "do this right."

He seemed equally perplexed. He looked toward the hall, then at the couch, then at her. "I've had dreams about this moment, Raine. To tell you the truth, I'm not sure that I'm not dreaming right now. But I hadn't planned on—" As if on cue he coughed again.

"You should probably lie down," Raine murmured solicitously. "After everything you've been through..." She tucked herself against his side and maneuvered under his arm. "I'll take you to bed."

Gabe gave a funny little laugh. "Now I know I'm dreaming."

They started down the hall. At the door to his room she paused before opening it.

"What did your doctor say?" she asked as they went inside.

"To take it easy for about a week."

She left him standing long enough to fold down the bed covers, then she went back to assist him.

"I'm not an invalid," he said.

"Let me take care of you."

She got him onto the side of the bed, but when she went to draw away, he stopped her.

"Lie with me," he requested huskily.

"I don't want to do anything that will make you worse."

"It'll be worse for me if you leave."

"But I'm not leaving," she assured him. "I told you—"

"I meant the room," he murmured, and gave her that special Gabe smile.

His hand slid slowly up her arm, and Raine had to shut her eyes to keep from crying out.

He drew her close to him.

"This feels so strange," she said.

"We're married."

"I know, but it still feels strange."

"I can make it feel better."

"Gabe—"

He gave a little turn and she was stretched out on the bed beside him.

"*I...love...you.*" He gave each word equal emphasis. "Not like a friend, not like a brother. Like this," he breathed as his lips left a trail of fire down her throat to the burgeoning curves of her breasts.

"Not a brother," Raine panted, echoing his theme. Her blood had started to sing a new song, one she had never heard before. "*Never* a brother!"

Gabe was exquisitely gentle as he made love to her. He coughed occasionally, but he wouldn't let the impairment stop him. It seemed to Raine as if he *had* to make love to her, not only to satisfy a physical need, but to assure himself that she was his. As if the moment that their bodies merged they would break a seal that could never be set in place again. The world, as they had known it, would be forced to shift in order to make way for a spectacular new universe.

"IF I DIE NOW, I'll die happy," Gabe murmured, spent, shortly after rolling onto his side.

Raine carefully smoothed the light film of moisture from his face and neck and couldn't resist letting her hand trail over his chest, ostensibly to perform

the same service. "I won't let you die," she murmured.

"You could be the cause," he teased.

Raine stretched, enjoying the uniqueness of being
in his bed. Who would have thought? Then she cud-
dled against Gabe. His long, leanly muscled body
was very pleasing to her. She loved the way it
moved, the way it felt, the way it looked.

His arm came around her and pulled her closer.
For a long time neither of them said anything. They
just lay there, reveling in what had happened.

Then Raine started to giggle. "I wonder what the
gossips would say if they knew."

"Heaven help us," Gabe rejoined.

"Mom's going to know in a New York second."

Gabe grimaced. "Could we please leave New
York out of this?"

"In a second, then. A plain, old, ordinary second."

"Thank you."

They lapsed into silence again, until Gabe murmured, "I still want to do this right."

Raine pushed up onto an elbow to look at him.
"You said that earlier. What do you mean?"

Gabe's clear blue eyes were earnest. "I want us
to get married again, Raine. Only this time, we'll
mean it. Before, it was so…"

"Bloodless?" she supplied.

"It might be real in law, but not in spirit. I didn't
feel that you…"

She waited for him to finish, and when he didn't,
she asked, "What?"

"I wasn't in your plans then, Raine. I was never
in your plans."

Some of the pain that Gabe had suffered at her hands through all the years she'd been busy looking for life in other places had slipped through in those words. The lament of the person left behind.

Raine's heart ached for him, but there was nothing she could do about the past. There was plenty she could do about the future, though.

"You're in my plans now, Gabe," she swore to him. "You always have been, only I didn't know it." She laid her cheek against the warm, damp skin of his chest and said, "Yes, we should get married again. Every year at this time, if you like. We're a part of each other, Gabe. When you hurt, I hurt. When you're happy, I'm happy. When—"

He cut her off by dragging her up his body. "When I need you..." he murmured huskily.

"...I need—" she started to answer, but his impatience made completing the sentiment impossible.

EPILOGUE

THE CHURCH WAS FILLED with people, all dressed in their Sunday best. The invitation had been extended to everyone in town. *Come join with us in a renewal of our vows.*

The ceremony wasn't intended to be formal. Raine wore a beautiful white suit, very stylish, if cut a little loosely. Gabe looked extremely handsome in a dark business suit. Marge and George were beaming, as was Charles Atwood, who had arrived home the week before to the surprising news that there would be another wedding. Richard Jensen was honorary best man and Britt Marshack honorary matron of honor. Flowers decorated the alter and Raine clutched a bouquet.

It couldn't have been more different from the first hastily arranged ceremony, Gabe thought. And when he glanced at Raine, it was to discover that she was already looking at him.

Love made her eyes glow, and a tender smile transformed her face beyond mere earthly beauty. It was enough to make him catch his breath.

They took turns repeating the words of commitment, meaning each and every one.

Then came the kiss. This time Gabe was ready. He folded Raine into his arms and put every ounce of his love into the tribute sealing their union. He continued to hold her, even as the organ burst forth triumphantly.

It took Richard, for once grinning widely, to break them apart.

Britt laughed, Raine giggled and Richard thumped Gabe on the back.

As they started down the aisle, the countless faces that greeted them were awash with joy, everyone reacting to their obvious bliss.

At the doors they burst out into the sunshine, and Gabe couldn't resist once again showing the world his happiness. He murmured, "Wait," to Raine and with an elated grin, planted another huge kiss on her lips.

"Gabe, you're wonderful!" she breathed when he let her go.

People streaming out around them laughed and made teasing comments. Then they started to throw handfuls of confetti.

Marge kissed them both, as did Gabe's father. George settled for a handshake with Gabe and a kiss on Raine's cheek.

An avalanche of good wishes followed them to the rented limousine. The crowd was invited to have cake and punch in the activity building. Gabe and Raine were off for their one-week honeymoon in the Bahamas, courtesy of their friends.

It was far different from the bleakness of the last time.

Far different in their prospects for the future.

Gabe and Raine and the baby.

Together.

Forever.

HOMETOWN REUNION

continues with

A Touch of Texas

by Kristine Rolofson

Here's a preview!

A TOUCH OF TEXAS

WHY DON'T YOU take Tex out for a walk?" Marina asked her son. "I took her this morning, but she likes the rain a lot more than I do."

"Yeah, sure." He put his jacket on, all the while asking the dog if she wanted to go out. Tex ran around in circles, wagging her tail, her toenails clicking on the linoleum floor, until Jon hooked her up to the leash. She waited impatiently for him to open the back door, then led him outside.

Marina turned, the smile still on her face, as she faced The Cowboy. She wished he wasn't quite so good-looking, in that earthy Western way. He caught her smile and the corners of his tilted. "Are we having dinner together tonight?"

"Tonight?"

"Yes," he said. "I remember asking you. Saturday. To dinner."

"Isn't it getting late?"

"It's only four o'clock. I could pick you up at seven."

"I don't think that's such a good idea." She handed him a plastic bag and watched as he cleaned up the mess.

"We've been through this before, Marina," he said, turning on the water and washing his very large, very brown hands.

She wanted to go out with him, she wanted to say yes, but there were other things to consider. Like the complications that could develop from dating anyone. Not that Clint Stanford was just "anyone." He was a special man. And then there was the problem of what Jon would say. So far he'd accepted Clint as a family acquaintance, a necessary evil. Lord only knew what her son would say if he knew she'd kissed The Cowboy. In the backyard, no less.

She didn't want to hurt Clint's feelings, so she thought quickly. "What if we cook the fish you caught? I'll put some potatoes in to bake and make a salad."

He looked amused, which surprised her. "Just the three of us, huh?" Marina handed him the towel that hung by the sink and he dried himself off. "That's not exactly the romantic dinner I had planned."

"Whatever happened to going out as friends?"

"I lied," he said, stepping closer. He put those large hands on her shoulders and looked down into her face. "I want to do this," he whispered, touching his lips to hers for a brief, enticing second. "And this," he added, pulling her closer to him so that her breasts touched his chest. He kissed her again, this time lingering long enough to send frissons of sensation throughout her spine.

"Nice," he murmured, lifting his head slightly.

"Jon—"

"Is walking the dog," he finished for her, nuzzling her lips with his, dropping his hands to her waist. "I knew that animal would come in handy."

She couldn't help it. She twined her arms around his neck and slanted her mouth for his kiss. Crazy, she knew, but she was unable to resist the solid warmth of his body against hers.

It had been a long time. She'd forgotten how hard a man's chest could be. He urged her lips apart, taking the kiss to a new level of sensation.

READER SERVICE™

The best romantic fiction direct to your door

Our guarantee to you...

The Reader Service involves you in no obligation
to purchase, and is truly a service to you!

There are many extra benefits including a free
monthly Newsletter with author interviews,
book previews and much more.

Your books are sent direct to your door
on 14 days no obligation home approval.

We offer huge discounts on selected books
exclusively for subscribers.

Plus, we have a dedicated Customer Care team
on hand to answer all your queries on
(UK) 020 8288 2888
(Ireland) 01 278 2062.

GEN/GU/1

Escape into

Just a few pages into any Silhouette® novel and you'll find yourself escaping into a world of desire and intrigue, sensation and passion.

Silhouette

Diana
Palmer

Beloved

Rebecca
YORK

Nowhere Man

The
Marriage
Bargain

Jennifer Mikels

A Husband
Waiting To Happen

MARIE FERRARELLA

▼™ SILHOUETTE®

GEN/SIL/RS

A thrilling mix of passion, adventure and drama

▼™ SILHOUETTE SENSATION®

If it's excitement and adventure you seek in your romances, then join these dynamic men and women who are unafraid to live life to the fullest in these complex and dramatic stories.

Let us carry you away on the tides of passion!

Four new titles are available every month from the

READER SERVICE™
on subscription

GEN/18/RS

▼™ SILHOUETTE
DESIRE ®

*Provocative,
sensual love stories for the
woman of today*

Capture the intensity of falling in
love in these fast-paced, intense
love stories with strong, rugged
heroes who are just *irresistible!*

Six new titles available every
month from the

READER SERVICE™
on subscription

GEN/22/RS

▼™ SILHOUETTE
SPECIAL EDITION ®

Satisfying, substantial and compelling romances packed with emotion.

Experience the drama of living and loving in the depth and vivid detail that only Special Edition™ can provide.
The sensuality can be sizzling or subtle but these are always very special contemporary romances.

Six new titles available every month from the
READER SERVICE™
on subscription

GEN/23/RS

Danger, deception and desire

▼™SILHOUETTE
INTRIGUE™

Enjoy these dynamic mysteries with a
thrilling combination of breathtaking
romance and heart-stopping suspense.
Unexpected plot twists and
page-turning writing will keep you
on the edge of your seat.

Four new titles every month
available from the
READER SERVICE™
on subscription

GEN/46/RS